Clean-Out

A Paul Kanner Mystery

by

J. D. Demetre

For my son Joseph and my wife Sara

May love and imagination fill your days

-Chapter 1-

The Broken Window

Shards of glass floated in all directions in slow motion as Paul Kanner tried to summon the will to escape from the scene of his crime. The slowly cascading tingles of glass on pavement were overtaken by the more urgent sounds of a police siren. Paul was rooted to the spot. Paul heard a familiar yet loathsome voice from the broken window.

'You lunatic! The coppers will put you away where you belong, Oddball!'

It was Cameron, his tormentor of the past three years. John Cameron had made Paul's life a misery from almost his first day at Hollenbeck High School in Greenwich. Being labelled a 'special

4

needs' student brought him much more attention than he needed, especially of the negative kind. Over the years, Paul had suffered a number of indignities at the hands of John Cameron, quite apart from the name-calling. He'd had glue put into his hair, live matches thrust into his trouser pocket, rude signs stuck to the back of his blazer and smelly substances (including a raw egg yolk) put into his rucksack. Cameron's latest vile action was the worst...writing obscene words in Paul's homework book...and you can guess who got blamed for this! This was the last straw and yet Paul could not think of a suitable act of reprisal to satisfy his need for revenge...at least, not until he found himself on Cameron's street and decided on impulse to smash an upstairs window in his house (a bit of a bonus that it was actually Cameron's bedroom window). Paul's reverie was broken by the sound of slamming car doors.

5

"Oi, you, stay where you are!"

Paul felt a vice-like grip on his shoulder as he was roughly spun round to face the long arm of the law, which in this instance happened to belong to Detective Sergeant Joe Bertolli, a somewhat unkempt and shambling giant of a man who seemed on the verge of collapsing from an excess of booze or fatigue.

"Alright son... I'm the police. Just calm down. You picked a fine time to smash a window, didn't you? Right under our noses when we were investigating the ...er.. burglary a few doors away. Now how about explaining to me why you decided to smash that window? Oh by the way, I should tell you my name... I'm Joe...er...Detective Sergeant Joe Bertolli...of the Metropolitan Police."

Paul couldn't bring himself to look at the policeman's face. It wasn't only his usual wariness of other people...it was something more this time.

He felt more alien than ever before, even alien to himself...he couldn't understand what possessed him to pick up that brick and smash that bedroom window. He certainly hadn't planned it. All Paul could remember was feeling very angry and upset at all the name-calling and nastiness that his Year 9 classmates had directed his way. Things were getting worse and he didn't know how to cope. But somehow, mysteriously, these thoughts led to him picking up a brick and hurling it with all his might at someone's bedroom window...and that someone happened to be his cruellest tormentor, John Cameron! How could he ever begin to explain this to himself, let alone to the police? His head bowed low, Paul shuffled on his feet, hoping the policeman would tire of his silence and let him go with a mild ticking off.

"What's your name, son?" asked Bertolli. His question was met with silence, so he changed tact again. "Where do you live? Come on, you've got to talk to me otherwise I'll have no choice but to..."

"The oddball's called Paul Kanner and he lives down the road on Bertram Street" came John Cameron's unsolicited pent-up response. He was dying to talk to the copper – all the coppers were ignoring him and paying way too much attention to Kanner. The oddball was always getting way too much attention as far as he was concerned and he reckoned this explained why he was odd-balling all over the place – not enough attention at home maybe? He continued in his quest to help the police with their enquiries –

"He's an Aspie and always doing weird stuff and getting into trouble. Put him in jail and we'd all be happier around here."

"And you are...?" intoned Bertolli, barely able to disguise the irritation in his voice.

"I'm John Cameron, victim of this oddball.

We're in the same class and he's always doing stuff like this."

"Why do you keep referring to him as an *'oddball'* all the time?" continued Bertolli, his irritation spreading through his face like a crimson rash.

"Like I told you, *SIR*, he's an Aspie, you know, odd with people."

"I've never heard of Aspie...it's some kind of kids' slang for something is it?"

Before Cameron could respond, Paul Kanner roused himself from his hypnotic state and trotted out an answer that could have (and actually did) come straight out of the pages of a medical dictionary...

"Aspie as in Asperger's Syndrome, which is what I have. This is a condition in which a person finds it difficult to understand other people's mental states and the motives they have for doing

9

things. It is related to autism but not as severe. Some people with Asperger's Syndrome are geniuses in one area like maths or music or science or art. But everyone with Asperger's finds it hard to tell whether someone is lying or joking or pretending and people get annoyed with us because we think differently and aren't on the same wavelength as others". He slowly raised his eyes and was surprised to see a smile on Joe Bertolli's face.

"Don't tell me...let me guess...your area of genius is smashing windows..." said the smiling face.

"No, I think ..." said Paul, struggling to think of an appropriate reply to the policeman's question.

"I'm only kidding son", added Bertolli, oblivious to the irony contained in his statement. "OK, so what are we going to do with you? Let's begin by giving you a lift home and on the way, you can give me your version of things. PC Simon Cohen will talk with your 'friend' John".

-Chapter 2-

Homecoming

Safely ensconced in the squad car, Paul tried to prepare himself for an onslaught of questions that the policeman was likely to fire at him. Detective Sergeant Joe Bertolli eased his long body beside Paul in the back of the car and gently pulled the door shut. He turned to face Paul, who averted his gaze as if by a reflex action.

"It's OK son...I just want a little chat with you to find out what went on back there...when you're ready, in your own time."

"Sorry?"

"Just tell me everything that happened, from the beginning...how did you end up on Granby Street?"

Paul nestled his ears in his hunched shoulders in an attempt to shut out the whole world. He breathed a sigh and began, slowly and hesitantly...

"I live round the corner at Bertram Street and needed to get out...out of the house... because dad was shouting. He's always shouting. He says he can never get through to me but I don't know what that means and he gets very upset when I ask him to explain. So off I went to get some peace and quiet. I walked to the end of my road and then right into Granby Street. I wasn't even thinking about Cameron – just wanted to walk as far and as fast as I could. At number 47, just three doors away from Cameron's house, I saw this man in the doorway just staring at me. The door was closed and it looked as though he was just leaving the house. He just stared at me and I got a funny feeling in my stomach. I just couldn't bring myself to walk past number 47...instead I turned round and walked back and round the corner. The man scared me so much that I couldn't stop myself from peeking round the corner to see if he was following me. Luckily he wasn't; he was walking in the other direction, towards the far end of Granby Street. When he was out of sight I walked slowly back along Granby Street. I wanted to test my bravery by walking past number 47. Instead, I was shaking like a leaf and noticed a bit of brick on the pavement outside Cameron's house. I bent down, picked it up and threw it at his house without thinking."

"Paul, do you think you could describe the man who came out of number 47?"

"Yes, he was about 40 years old. He was quite short – about the same height as my dad, who is 5' 7". He was quite skinny. He had very short hair so that he looked bald. He had blue jeans that looked very new. He had a dark blue fleece jacket that had the words 'North Face' on the left breast written in silver and under that he wore a green T-shirt with yellow writing that said 'Born to Rock'. He had grey trainers with a light blue tick on the outer sides of the shoes. His socks were pink and I thought that was strange because everyone says men don't wear pink...and he was carrying an orange carrier bag that was full of cloths or dusters of some kind...lots of them and they were all a sort of dark yellow colour. In his left hand, he carried a small bottle wrapped in a carrier bag and some keys dangling from his fingers."

"My goodness Paul, you are observant!" said Joe Bertolli in a gravelly voice as his head reeled at the implications of what Paul had just described to him. "Come on, let's get you home...number 29 wasn't it?"

"Yes, round the corner and fifteen houses down on the left of the road."

Within seconds, they arrived outside Paul's

home. As they both approached the front gate, the door to the house swung open and out came an irate Mr Kanner, crimson-faced with rage.

"What are you doing with my boy?"

"Mr Kanner I presume? I'm Detective Sergeant Joe Bertolli sir."Bertolli showed his warrant card and exchanged bewildered looks with Paul's dad.

"The police? What's he done? He doesn't usually cause trouble...at least not outside the house!"

"Paul smashed a window of a classmate's house in Granby Street."

"Oh Christ, what did you do that for? Is it one of your more unfriendly classmates?"

Paul hunched his shoulders up as high as they would go and tried to disappear from the world yet again.

"Mr Kanner, I think I can see a way of

resolving this without any official action being taken against Paul. I have reason to believe that Paul can help us with another of our enquiries."

"Christ Paul, you're a right one aren't you... a fully fledged member of the criminal fraternity!"

"No sir, let me explain...Paul will be helping us as an innocent eyewitness in a burglary case...with your consent of course."

"Be my guest Sergeant!"

"Well, I'd best be off now so that Paul can at least have a normal evening after such an eventful day. May I please take down your 'phone number so that I can make arrangements with you regarding interviewing Paul?"

As Mr Kanner reeled off his 'phone number, Paul stared uncomprehendingly at the front door of his own house. What burglary case was the policeman talking about?

-Chapter 3-
Second Meeting

It was a breezy Saturday morning when Detective Sergeant Joe Bertolli drew up next to number 29 Bertram Street in his off-white Ford Capri. When he first bought this as an almost-new car it had been the one source of pride and joy in his life. He ambled to the front door of the Kanners' house and rang the doorbell. A careworn Mrs Kanner opened the door and hesitated in the doorway....

"May I please come in Mrs Kanner? I think your husband has informed you of the appointment I made to see Paul..."

"Oh..yes, of course...do come in".

Mrs Kanner showed the detective into the living room and asked if he'd like a cup of tea, which he politely declined. She offered him a seat and called up to Paul...

"Paul.........Pauuuuuuuuul.......the policeman is here to talk to youuuuuuuuuuuu!" Paul stampeded down the stairs without a reply. He smiled weakly at Joe Bertolli and surprised himself by realising that he was actually glad to see the detective. Mrs Kanner excused herself and left Paul and the detective to themselves.

"Hi Paul!"

"Oh hi...um..."

"It's alright, you can call me Joe. How have you been since last week?"

"OK, just the usual...school and stuff."

"Any more incidents with John Cameron?"

"Nothing special...just the annoying name-calling."

"Have your parents spoken to the teachers about this?" Paul shrugged his shoulders in a way that told the detective that this topic was off-limits.

"Well anyway Paul, I wanted you to know that I've talked to my chief inspector about you and she's agreed to your being given a verbal warning about last weekend's episode, on the grounds of your having been distressed by seeing a burglary suspect. So, no ASBO, no interview at the station....and...." - Bertolli assumed a sly and hesitant smile..."no prison either, at least not for now!"

Paul was very perplexed by Joe Bertolli's latest pronouncements and struggled to keep himself from swooning. The detective noticed his disquiet and patted him on the shoulder. "Listen Paul, you don't need to worry. I think you can help us with a burglary case...the man you saw in Granby Street was in all likelihood the burglar we call Mr Sheen, who has been at large for over ten years and this might be the closest we get to catching him. He seems to prey on unoccupied houses in South-East London owned by wealthy people. His M.O. is to steal the valuables, then go back and give the place a thorough clean...the owners are often quite disconcerted to find a dust-free shiny (but empty) home when they return."

"What is M.O.? " was Paul's only response.

"Oh, modus operandi...Latin, meaning typical way of doing things...or his own personal style, if you like."

Paul stared into the distance and was lost in thought. He turned his eyes in the general direction of the detective and looked solemn. He then turned his focus away from the detective as he started to analyse what he had been told and spoke as if to himself.

"This Mr Sheen man sounds very odd. I mean, why does he go back to clean a house *after* he has stolen everything from it? Wouldn't it be better if

21

he cleaned up while he was already there – you know, got rid of fingerprints and fibres and stuff...and DNA from any of his hairs that might have fallen? If he cleaned up straight away there'd be less chance that he'd be caught as well. Does he have a special reason or is it that he can't help himself? Maybe he cleans up both times, when he's there to steal and also the second time when he lets himself in with the keys he stole the first time. I don't understand it."

Joe Bertolli cast a wary glance in Paul's direction, not wishing to intrude on his thought processes.

"Paul, we at the Met are also puzzled by this. My boss, Chief Inspector Sara Gravesham thinks this guy is simply trying to confuse us, but I'm not so sure. He could confuse us just by carrying on getting away with the burglaries; he obviously chooses his targets meticulously and plans his return visits so as to evade capture. I guess he must spend a lot of time skulking around a neighbourhood and taking note of people's movements in the vicinity of the target house. He obviously also knows a thing or two about police procedures in this situation. But one thing that we do know about him for sure is that he is a very dangerous and cunning man. I don't want to tell you too much about him right now, except to say that he paints some rather sinister messages on the walls of the houses he burgles. In one house in Blackheath where the burglary fits Mr Sheen's M.O., we found a message on a living- room wall that said: 'You can hide but I will find you in the dust'. In the alley at the back of this house we found the broken remnants of a camera and a pair of smashed spectacles. On the same day, an estate agent who had been taking photos in that neighbourhood was found unconscious two streets away in a crumpled heap.

You have to wonder what kind of a man we're dealing with here..."

The detective had at this point expended all of his energy and fell into a brooding silence. Paul felt a twinge of pity for this lumbering man who had actually paid attention to what he had had to say. Paul was also grateful to Bertolli for giving him a sense of purpose and excitement through his involvement in the case. Since that fateful day when he had met Joe Bertolli, Paul felt happy and fulfilled for the first time in years. He 'owed one' to Joe and resolved to help the detective in his quest to outwit and capture Mr Sheen.

"Erm...did Mr Sheen leave a message at number 47 Granby Street?"

"Yes Paul. On one of the living- room walls, he had painted the message: I WILL TAKE BACK WHAT IS MINE!"

"I wonder if he thinks someone has stolen

something from *him*?"

"I don't know Paul...something tells me that we are dealing with something more complicated than a crackpot on the loose".

Paul nervously stole a glance at Bertolli's face and then withdrew into a quiet corner of his mind where he contemplated the mystery that was Mr Sheen. His reverie was cut short by the yappy arrival of his brown and black Yorkshire terrier/poodle, Bella. Paul always felt comforted by Bella's presence and her playful antics distracted him from whatever was bothering him. He was still gloomy after a particularly bad day at school yesterday. Not only had he fallen victim to one of Cameron's violent outbursts (his bruised ribs were still a reminder of this), but his form tutor had also been particularly unpleasant, accusing Paul of being self-centred, impolite and a waste of space, just because Paul had pointed out, contrary to Mr Tonnack's claims, that acids had low numbers on the pH scale. Bella had always been Paul's first port of call after any school-day that had been marred by bully Cameron and his cronies or idiotic teachers...she always sensed when he was unhappy, unlike his parents, who usually told him that he had to try to be strong.

Joe Bertolli was about to bid farewell to Paul and Bella, when he checked himself, and quietly and intently gazed at Paul's face. He suspected that Paul was a troubled young man and he could see that at this moment in time Paul's mind should be allowed to escape amid the playful affections of his Yorkiepoo Bella. He crept out of the house unnoticed by Paul and his family.

-Chapter 4-

A Meeting of Minds

Detective Sergeant Joe Bertolli had spent the whole of his Sunday in an agitated state. His boss, Inspector Sara Gravesham, had as recently as Friday night reminded him that it was *his* job to solve the Mr Sheen burglaries. The 'Mr Sheen Case' had been on the Metropolitan Police case-file for over ten years and it was now widely regarded by the news media and police alike as insoluble. The case-file always seemed to land on the desk of the detective who was least liked by the top brass and it was little surprise that it had sat on Joe Bertolli's desk for the past six months. Whilst considered as highly intelligent and highly capable by his superiors, Joe Bertolli was one of the least popular of all of the

27

detectives working for the Met. He was a loner who disliked small-talk and banter and held colleagues and superiors alike in contempt. Many thought him to be arrogant and aloof and enjoyed seeing him fail. The Mr Sheen case had been obsessing him for months and he was determined to uncover the identity of this mysterious burglar. Paul Kanner might hold the key to this mystery, but he had to tread very carefully with this vulnerable boy.

On Monday morning, Joe Bertolli awoke before his alarm went off and resolved to see his friend, Dr Benjamin Zeigarnik, the police psychologist. Dr Zeigarnik was the only colleague whom Joe could confide in and he would often see him to get his perspective on a difficult case. Over the past two years, the two men had become friends, enjoying each other's quirky humour and intelligence. Zeigarnik was often consulted by the Met when they needed to work out the possible motives of criminals in unsolved cases. Knowing about what motivated a particular crime – greed, envy, jealousy, passion, could often give clues about likely suspects. On Mondays and Fridays, Zeigarnik worked at the University of London, where he had a small forensic psychology laboratory and an even smaller office.

Joe Bertolli made his way to the University's Bloomsbury campus in central London, climbed the interminable stairs of Senate House and knocked on the office door of his friend. Dr Zeigarnik, a big, bearded and imposing man opened the door and greeted Joe with a warm smile.

"Joe my friend, fancy seeing you here! I was beginning to think that you had solved the Mr Sheen case without me!"

"You're a very funny man Benjamin, and this is the reason for my visit – I need a good laugh. As to solving the Mr Sheen case, you haven't been of much help in the past six months, so why do you think I would come to see you about it?"

"OK, so, you've fallen in love with your boss and you've come to see your friendly psychologist for advice, eh? I can only say that I strongly advise you against proposing marriage to Chief Inspector Sara Gravesham, who is likely to..."

"Let's get down to business Benjamin. We now have a witness who confirms our earlier suspicion that Sheen *returns* to the crime scene to *clean* the property. The witness is a teenage boy who seems to have sharp observational skills and..."

"Seems to have...how do you know?"

"He has Asperger's Syndrome and I've read that these kids notice details that are normally missed by other people...is this right?"

"Yes, but maybe I should meet this witness to assess him. Maybe what he said to you comes from a movie or a dream. Who knows, people with

Asperger's don't always make the most reliable witnesses."

"OK Benjamin, I'll arrange a meeting. In the meantime, there are many puzzling features in this case that I'd like to review with you…"

Dr Zeigarnik stared in response, his face forming an exaggerated scowl. "You think I have time to chat on a Monday morning? What about my research for the university, what about my research for the Met, what about my…*work*!? OK, let me make us some coffee first."

Armed with steaming mugs of coffee, the two men leaned toward each other and sighed in unison. Bertolli and Zeigarnik had shared many previous 'meeting of minds' sessions and both were feeling like hamsters in a running-wheel. As usual, Bertolli summarised the Mr Sheen case – a number of burglaries in the past ten years had these common characteristics:

1.   The burglar cleared out the whole house, taking everything that wasn't screwed to the floor or too heavy to carry;

2.   The burglar targeted expensive properties;

3.   The burglar returned on a separate occasion to give the property he'd just burgled a thorough clean and polish. The young lad Paul Kanner must have seen him coming out of number 47 Granby Street literally hours after the burglary. On that morning, the police had received a call from a neighbour saying that on the previous night, she had seen an unmarked van screeching away at some speed. On the following morning, she checked through the bay window of number 47 and noticed that

an armchair was missing. That's when she called the police. When uniforms checked the place, it was virtually empty, with the exception of beds, wardrobes and cupboards;

4.   The time interval between the first and second visits varied each time, from several hours after the police had been alerted to several weeks afterward;

5.   A canister of *Mr Sheen* furniture polish was often found in the vicinity of the property;

6.   Cryptic messages were always painted on one of the interior walls, which only sometimes made sense to the police and only afterwards, when some other crime had been committed;

7.   Unusually for this kind of

serial crime, none of the stolen items was ever recovered and there were no leads;

8.   One new thing - if Paul is a reliable witness, the police now have a make on the criminal – about 40 years of age, white, on the short side, skinny, with closely cropped hair;

9.   The profile of the criminal, his motives and reasons, are totally elusive – detectives and psychologists alike have struggled to piece together a plausible theory about this man.

Dr Benjamin Zeigarnik took a sharp intake of breath and let out a trilling whistling sound between his gritted teeth. "Look Joe, we need to look at these characteristics from a fresh angle. So far, we have focused our theories mainly on the criminal's bizarre return visits and his indiscriminate ransacking of houses, taking many items that are worthless along with the more valuable items. I have already explained to you what these peculiarities might mean...the value of these items is probably to do with reminders of his own childhood home...maybe an early part of his life that was happy and normal. The knick-knacks that he steals might be just as important to him as the expensive stuff that he takes from the houses. I would guess that he lives alone and is quite lonely and has few mementos of childhood and family life. In all likelihood, we are dealing with someone who has experienced a string of fostering placements and other forms of early instability. ..but then again, this background is hardly unusual in criminals. No, if we want to find out something distinctive and useful about this man, we need to focus more on the messages he leaves on the walls..."

-Chapter 5-

Time to Play

Bertolli left Dr Zeigarnik's office with a spinning head and an escalating feeling of helplessness. His instinct was to run a mile from Zeigarnik's psychobabble and get his teeth into something solid. Maybe it was time to renew hope by visiting his star witness... his only witness, Paul Kanner. He needed to be sure that Paul really was a reliable witness. Maybe he could check out Paul's powers of observation and memory.

When he pulled up in his car at Bertram Street, Bertolli found that the parking space next to Paul's house was empty. He wondered whether Paul was out with his parents in their car. He decided to try the front door in any case. He squeezed out of his tight-fitting car and lumbered toward the front gate of Paul's house.

The gate latch was stuck with rust and Bertolli yanked at it with all his might...which was not sufficient to impress the stubborn gate latch. He decided to jump over the gate..."That was great, haven't done the high jump in years", he said to himself. Bertolli landed just a few feet from the Kanners' front door and as he did so, the front door opened very slowly.

"Oh, hello Mrs Kanner...I wondered if I could have a chat with your Paul...he has been really helpful with my burglary case."

"Yes sergeant, come in. I'm sure he'd be very pleased to see you."

Paul appeared in the living room with the yapping Bella and sat on the sofa across from the already seated detective.

"How's tricks, Paul?"

"Umm...fine...have you caught Mr Sheen yet?"

"No such luck. Your account is all we have to go on...and that's why I'm here Paul, to check out your story."

"It wasn't a story...it was what I saw. That man in Granby Street with the bag full of yellow cloths and..."

"Look Paul, I believe you...it's just that you were very upset that day and sometimes how we feel affects the way we see and remember things".

"Does it?" Bella nuzzled into Paul's leg, sensing the tension in Paul's voice.

"It can do. Look, supposing you are in a fun mood and feeling really happy and you see a man coming out of a house with a bag. What might you think is going on? Because you are in a good mood you might think the man is nice and that maybe he lives there and you wouldn't bother paying any attention to his clothes. But if you were in a bad mood, you might see things differently...that this man is up to no good and so you look longer at him and notice everything about him. The thing is, was it Mr Sheen you saw or some relative of the house owner? The incredible detail you gave me about this man might be to do with the fact that you were in a bad mood and saw the man as a bad guy...do you see what I mean?"

Paul looked lost in thought and replied hesitantly..."Not really...umm...I don't understand why you see differently at different times...my brain doesn't work like that."

Bertolli scratched his head and tried to come up with a strategy to check out this remarkable boy's memory.

"I have an idea...do you have a Monopoly set?"

"Yes, it's one of my favourite games, though I

like chess best."

"OK then, bring it over and we can play on this table".

Pursued by a highly excited Bella, Paul went upstairs to his room to fetch the game, all the while feeling perplexed by the odd policeman's words. He wondered what point Bertolli was trying to make about seeing and remembering things differently when your mood was different, and he could not make sense of this. Maybe detectives have a special way of dealing with kids because they think kids just make everything up. Maybe the detective was trying to confuse him...but he seems so nice.

As the minutes passed, Bertolli lost patience and called up to Paul. "Hey Paul, have you found the Monopoly set yet?" He was answered by a succession of barks and growls before Paul could even begin to reply.

"Yes, coming down now."

Paul set up the Monopoly board and chose the car piece for himself. Bertolli chose the boot.

"OK Paul, let's play. I'll have you know that I used to be the South-East London Monopoly champion back in the day!"

"Wow, really?" replied Paul haltingly and betraying his scepticism about Bertolli's prowess with the game. After twenty minutes of playing, it became abundantly clear to Paul that the detective was ruthless in his play, but was nonetheless losing to Paul, who went about the game in a quiet, almost disinterested way.

"Your turn...umm...Sergeant..."

"Paul, remember you can call me Joe. Now before I take my turn, I'd like you to answer a question for me. Did you notice anything unusual about how I threw the dice?"

"Mmm...yes, you changed the hand you used on each turn...umm...you threw the dice with your left hand to begin with, then with your right hand and then you kept changing hands each turn."

"Well, well, well...you are very observant Paul."

"So...umm...you believe me now? I mean...about what I saw in Granby Street?"

"Paul, I've always believed you, but I just wanted to make sure. We always have to be a little sceptical of what witnesses think they have seen."

"Oh...umm...I noticed something else that was odd about your turns. You rolled three doubles in your fifteen rolls of the dice: a double 1 followed by a double 3 followed by a double 5."

Bertolli's jaw hung limply as he stared at Paul for some seconds before his face contorted to reveal the mixture of awe, surprise, joy and even fear that he felt. He himself had not noticed how many doubles he had thrown, let alone their value or the fact that he had taken fifteen turns.

"Did I really?", he replied in a resigned way. His thoughts ran along an entirely different path: *I'd better get Zeigarnik to look at this lad...he'll be able to test his abilities more objectively!*

"Paul, do you like doing science at school?"

"Yes, it's the only thing that's good about school. I also like doing experiments at home...you know, making little explosions and creating goopy stuff with chemicals...but my parents are not all that keen. I keep telling then that I want to be a scientist when I'm older, but they don't seem very interested."

Bertolli noticed how Paul's broad grin had faded into a sullen frown as soon as he mentioned his parents. "OK then, how would you like to meet a scientist who is an expert on memory? He's a good friend of mine and you'll be able to do some fun experiments with him."

"OK..."

"Let's go and talk to your parents about this and get their permission. We'll visit him at his lab on Monday...his name is Dr Benjamin Zeigarnik by the way. At least you won't be bored playing with your video games on the bank holiday!"

Paul cast a bemused glance at Bertolli before he replied. "But I'm never bored playing with my PlayStation."

-Chapter 6-

Testing Times

The Ford Capri screeched to a juddering halt outside the gates of London University's Senate House. The seven-mile journey from Greenwich proved to be anything but straightforward: the car's brakes were on the point of failure and the engine stalled on two occasions. To cap it all, the exhaust pipe created an unexpected and extraordinarily loud bang as it backfired near Tower Bridge, which led to an elderly cyclist falling off her bike. Joe Bertolli wearily got out of the car and made his way to the other side to help Paul out of his decrepit seat. Just as Paul began to struggle out of the car, Bertolli was accosted by a traffic warden.

"Excuse me sir. You can't park here, it's a

restricted zone."

Bertolli fished into his coat pockets and eventually found his police warrant card, which he proudly displayed to the scowling traffic warden. "Look, I'm here on urgent police business. I need to be in that building for the next several hours where I'll be conducting an investigation."

With a gleam in his eye, the traffic warden pointed to the sign on the gate: NO PARKING ON ANY ACCOUNT. GATE IN CONSTANT USE. "I'm sorry sir, you have to move your car!"

"Come on Paul, get in the car. Let's find a more hospitable spot to park in." The Ford Capri drove round the streets of Bloomsbury in search of a legitimate parking space and in the process getting further and further away from Senate House. Eventually, Bertolli found a suitable spot in a narrow lane near Charing Cross Station. The twenty-minute walk to Dr Zeigarnik's building did little to improve Joe Bertolli's mood. By this time, Paul had also become quite agitated and started to withdraw into himself. The journey was quite challenging for Paul, not so much because of the various mishaps that had occurred, but because of having to spend so much time amongst unfamiliar streets, sounds and smells...a long way from the relative calm of the Greenwich streets he knew.

As the lift-doors were emblazoned with an "OUT OF ORDER" sign, Joe and Paul trudged their way wearily up the stairs of Senate House until they came upon the seventh floor office of Dr Benjamin Zeigarnik. Just as Joe was steeling himself to knock on the door, the door swung open and out popped the grizzled head of Benjamin Zeigarnik.

"Ahhh...by the twitching of my beard, if this is not the timely arrival of my esteemed colleague, Sergeant Joe Bertolli! Greetings! I have been expecting you...for at least an hour! Did you find it difficult to wake up or has that cheap Taiwanese watch of yours packed up?"

"Funny man", retorted Bertolli, as he grunted his way into the office, Paul trailing behind him, his head cowed as if trying to duck under some kind of barrier.

Zeigarnik glanced at Paul with a kindly expression. "You must be Paul" he said in a much gentler tone than he used when interacting with adults, who on the whole, tended to be a source of irritation and disappointment to him. Zeigarnik extended his left hand to Paul in a limp, tentative and unobtrusive way, as though wary of spooking the boy. Paul extended his own left hand and gently shook Zeigarnik's.

"Hah, another lefty...the best people in the world are left-handed" was Zeigarnik's jubilant response.

"Are they?" asked Paul distractedly.

"Well, at least you and I are both left-handed!" replied Zeigarnik, with mild amusement in his eyes. Paul's brief glimpse in Zeigarnik's direction betrayed a level of bemusement as the boy puzzled over the psychologist's intentions. Being an experienced psychologist, Dr Zeigarnik realised very quickly that he needed to put the increasingly alarmed Paul at ease.

"Paul, can I get you a Coke or an apple juice or an orange juice or a tea or a coffee?"

"Urm...Coke, please."

"And have you had breakfast...how about some sweet pastries?"

"Yes, I always have to have breakfast before I go out. Yes please, I'd like a pastry."

"What about you Joe, can I get you anything?"

"A black coffee please...and make it strong."

Zeigarnik raised an index finger skyward in dramatic fashion and with two long strides disappeared through the adjoining door to his laboratory. He quickly returned with a can of Coke, an apple-turnover pastry and a mug of steaming coffee.

"How rude of me Paul, I haven't properly introduced myself. My name is Benjamin and I'm a psychologist. Do you know what a psychologist is?"

"Urm...someone who studies people and how they think and helps with people's problems?"

"Exactly right! Now Joe here tells me that you may have seen a man that the police call Mr Sheen. He also tells me that you are good at remembering things..."

"Some things I can remember...colours, shapes and things...not so good with remembering reasons for stuff or people's faces."

"OK, well if you like, once you've finished eating and drinking and have relaxed a little, I'd like to show you some videos so we can see what you can remember. Are you OK with this?" Paul nodded in response.

Before entering the lab with all the video equipment and other gizmos, Zeigarnik cast a glance at the reclining figure of Joe Bertolli. "Will you care to join us Joe, or would you prefer to catch up on your beauty sleep?"

"I'll be right there Benjamin. Just need to call the station first."

The three figures entered the lab which was considerably bigger than the office and more dimly lit. Joe perched himself on a stool near the entrance, while Paul looked at the walls around the room which were festooned with trailing electrical wires, pictures of the brain and graphs with squiggly lines. Lowering his gaze, he could see video equipment on a bench as well as several devices that he did not recognise. His facial expression was one of awe.

51

"OK Paul, before we begin, let's have a bit of fun with all of this scientific equipment...Joe tells me you like science, so let's see what you think of this stuff."

With rising excitement, Paul stared at the equipment that took up every square inch of workbench surface in the lab: shiny consoles with read-out meters; three computer screens, one of which displayed an array of stills of dodgy-looking women's faces; two minuscule video-cameras mounted on oversized tripods; wires connected to push-button devices...and best of all, a PlayStation console.

Benjamin Zeigarnik could tell from one glance at Paul that he was hooked. "Paul, let me tell you about my favourite piece of equipment. This one here is what we call a polygraph." Zeigarnik pointed to a laptop connected by electrical leads to various curious attachments, including a large plastic-looking wide ring, rubber straps and little rubber rings. Zeigarnik typed some commands into the laptop and four squiggly lines appeared on the screen. "When these gizmos are attached to your body, the computer can show you how excited you are. See this line here, it's produced from this strap, which we call a pneumograph, which goes around a person's chest, and measures how rapidly they are breathing. The more excited the person is, the more zig-zags you get in that line. That line there comes from this big ring that we call a sphygmograph, which is worn around the upper-arm and measures how fast the person's blood is flowing. The more excited the person is, the more zig-zags you get on *that* line. These other two lines come from other devices that measure the person's pulse-rate and how sweaty their hands are. So why do you think I would want to find out how excited someone is?"

Paul gazed absent-mindedly at Dr Zeigarnik's

beard as though mesmerised. He marvelled at those squiggly lines on the computer screen and didn't really think there had to be a reason behind all this. "Um...is it because it is easier to see how excited someone is than it is to ask them?" he said with a slight tremor in his voice.

"Yes, well done Paul...and the other thing that some scientists believe is that in some situations, people show excitement when they are lying! Some scientists use the polygraph as a kind of lie-detector. Let me show you. Just to save time, let's just connect you to the pneumograph. Just let me know when the belt is comfortably tight around your chest. Now that you are OK with this Paul, I'm going to ask you three questions and I want you to answer truthfully. With the fourth question, I want you to lie by telling me the answer is "no". OK, have you got that?"

As soon as Paul nodded, Zeigarnik looked at

the screen which showed one squiggly line coming from the pneumograph. "OK Paul, now relax..." After a few minutes, the line on the screen became smoother as Paul became less nervous of the situation. "Now Paul, I'm going to ask those four questions now..."

"Is your name Peter Frith?"

"No."

"Are you an old man?"

"No."

"Do you live in New York City?"

"No."

"Are you a male?"

"Er...erm...no."

The line on the screen became quite zig-zaggy as soon as Paul started to answer this final question, whereas the line was smoother when he had answered the first three questions. Paul looked at Zeigarnik with something like awe on his face.

"I see you are impressed Paul! Now let me tell you a little bit more about this. Have you heard of Wonder Woman?"

"You mean the superhero?"

"Yes! Well, the man who created the Wonder Woman comic-books was a psychologist called Dr William Marston...and you know what, he was also one of the first people to use a pneumograph like the one we've just used. Now tell me, what special weapons did Wonder Woman have?"

"Erm...a sort of rope that she caught people in and it made them tell the truth...erm...and some magical bracelets?"

"Yes, the rope that you mentioned was called the Lasso of Truth...and guess what? William Marston's idea for this was inspired by the belt that you're now wearing around your chest...because he believed that the pneumograph could be used to detect if a person was lying."

Paul looked puzzled. "But Wonder Woman's lasso forced people to tell the truth...isn't that a bit different?"

"Yes, you're right Paul. Dr Marston's creation of the lasso was inspired by the pneumograph, but in real life he hadn't figured out how to force people to tell the truth...I guess it was one of his fantasies to achieve this one day." Paul slowly nodded his head as he tried to grapple with the implications of what Benjamin Zeigarnik had just told him.

Dr Zeigarnik allowed Paul to look around the lab and answered various questions about the equipment as well as the graphs and other figures that were displayed on the walls. Zeigarnik was very pleased by Paul's interest in the lab. Sensing that Paul was ready for some new activities, Zeigarnik clicked on a laptop and an image appeared of a group of young people with a basketball. "Now

Paul, in a minute, I'm going to show you a video of some kids playing with a basketball. Three of them are wearing a white T-shirt and the other three are wearing a black T-shirt. I want to find out how good your concentration level is. I would like you to focus only on the players dressed in white and at the end of the video I'm going to ask you to tell me how many times these guys passed the ball to each other. Got it?"

Paul stared intently at the screen as young people bounced and threw a basketball. Focusing on the white-clad figures, he kept count of all the passes they had made. Quite suddenly and confusingly, a gorilla appeared on the scene and appeared to walk out of camera-shot, unnoticed by the players. Paul had to concentrate hard on the players to ensure he didn't lose count of the number of passes they made with the ball.

Benjamin Zeigarnik paused the video when it

had reached the end and looked at Paul in a mock-challenging manner. "So Paul, let's find out how well you did...how many times did the kids in white pass the ball?".

"Fifteen?"

"Excellent! Now tell me, did you see anything unusual in that video clip?"

"Erm...a gorilla...or a man dressed as a gorilla walked by the players, but I don't think they saw him."

"Well done Paul. Do you know that most people don't notice the gorilla in the video?" Paul responded with a puzzled expression. "Now, if you don't mind, I'd like us to see a few more videos to see how good your memory is. But before we do this, how about I take you and your sleeping policeman out for lunch and then we can resume our tests? I hope you don't mind spending your Bank Holiday Monday helping the police with their enquiries!"

Paul nodded uncertainly just as Joe Bertolli fell from his stool with a grunt. Benjamin Zeigarnik rolled his eyes heavenward, shook his head and grabbed his office keys from the desk. "Follow me!" he barked at Paul and Joe.

-Chapter 7-

Too Much to Swallow

Dr Zeigarnik led the way to his favourite restaurant, Café Roma on Great Russell Street. As soon as they entered, he was greeted by an effusive Italian voice. "Benji, Benji, how you doing my friend? It is so good to see you. Welcome, welcome, welcome! Who are your friends?"

"Greetings Luigi, this is Sergeant Joe Bertolli."

"Ah, you must be Italian with a name like that!"

Joe smiled warmly at Luigi. "Yes, both my parents are from Naples, but I was born here in London and barely speak a word of Italian. This is Paul, who is helping us with our research."

Luigi looked at all three customers as though

they were long-lost members of his own family. "Welcome to all of you. It is good to have you here...come, sit over here at the window table. I will get you some menus right away."

Paul ordered a pepperoni and mushroom pizza while Joe and Benjamin plumbed for the spaghetti carbonara. All three waited for their food in silence...Paul because he was consumed with hunger, Joe and Benjamin because they were wracking their brains to think of a suitable topic of conversation that would engage the youngster. The food arrived and Paul attacked his pizza with gusto. Benjamin Zeigarnik was the first to break the silence. "How are you Paul, are you enjoying your pizza?"

"Umm...yes, thank you."

"You know Paul, this place is very special to me. Luigi was like a substitute father to me when I first moved here from Russia thirty years ago. Luigi is a fascinating man...not only an exquisite chef who runs his own business, but also a renowned historian before he fully retired from the university...Doctor Luigi Pecorino. He was the first person to discover that the Romans believed that different kinds of foods had an impact on mood and thinking. His book on the subject, *Roman Foodlore*, is very entertaining and informative and won him several awards."

Paul gazed at Dr Zeigarnik's beard with an ever-widening smile. "I'm very interested in the Romans. I read a book last week on the Roman gods..." Luigi overheard Paul's remark on his way back from the kitchen. He smiled benevolently at Paul and said "You are a wonderful young man...Roman history is so fascinating!"

"So Paul, what else are you interested in?" interjected Joe Bertolli.

"Mainly things that I can do on my own. I read

a lot, I like doing science experiments and I have a microscope and a telescope that I use quite a lot...and I like computer chess and video games."

"And are you still having problems with bullying in school?"

"Not so much now...I think John Cameron and his cronies have become a bit bored with trying to torment me and since my involvement with the police, the teachers are watching over me more."

An awkward silence followed which was broken by Benjamin Zeigarnik inquiring whether anyone wanted dessert. "I can't eat any more, thanks" said Paul. Joe's response was to rub his stomach soothingly and groan. "Right then, back to the lab gentlemen!" barked Zeigarnik.

After Zeigarnik paid the bill and he and Luigi embraced in a bear-hug he led the way to the lab at Senate House. After such a heavy meal, all three struggled to climb the seven flights of stairs to

Zeigarnik's office and lab. When they reached the landing, they saw a man looking quite edgy as he stared at Zeigarnik's office door. Before Zeigarnik could ask him what he wanted, the man bolted down the stairs and was quickly out of sight.

"I wonder what he wanted?" asked Joe.

"I have no idea...probably a student running late for an appointment who lost his way."

Once they were inside the now-familiar confines of the lab and Joe Bertolli had resumed his comfortable spot on the stool, Zeigarnik introduced Paul to the next test. He proceeded to show in succession two five-minute videos. The first video depicted a woman and two men walking past a series of shops. The woman entered some of the shops and the two men separately entered some of the other shops. The second video showed another woman and another two men walking along a different street, with each person going into some of the shops but not others. Once Paul had finished watching the videos, Zeigarnik asked him to play the card game *Go Boom* with him. Zeigarnik explained the rules: try to get rid of your cards by matching the suit or number of your opponent's card. After they had been playing for a few minutes, Paul asked the obvious question: "Why are we playing this game...is it a test? Will you be asking me questions about what I remember from those two videos?"

"I will be testing you to see how accurate your memory is for the events shown in the two videos. We're playing this little card game to give your brain a chance to forget some of the things you saw in the videos...and playing a game also stops you from reviewing the material in your head. I like my tests to be thorough!"

After a few more minutes, Zeigarnik began to probe Paul's memory, asking questions about the six people in the two videos and their actions: what they were wearing, colour of hair, facial expressions, what shops each person visited in the videos and also their mood when they came out of the shop. Zeigarnik was very encouraged by Paul's performance.

"Well Paul, you have a first-rate memory for clothing, hair-colour and shops visited by each person...but not so good with remembering the facial expressions or moods of the six people." In fact, Paul answered "I don't know" to all the questions about the six characters' facial expressions and moods. "I think you deserve a Coke for all your fine work", he said, handing Paul a chilled bottle. "I'll have a quick word with Joe and come back to you with one very short test and then we're done."

Zeigarnik strode to the lumbering figure perched on the stool and tapped him on the shoulder. "You can wake up now Joe, we've almost finished."

"Urgh...so tired...urm...how did Paul do on your tests?"

"He did very well, and just as I would have expected of an intelligent boy with Aspergers. He had perfect recall of all events, but was very poor with facial expressions and moods. I would say he's potentially a reliable witness to what happened on Granby Street that day, provided you're not relying on him to remember anything to do with the mood of the potential Mr Sheen character. But I have one more simple test for him...perhaps you'd care to join us."

Zeigarnik and Bertolli strode over to Paul, who was happily nursing his bottle of Coke. "Now Paul, you will recall that when we returned to my office we saw someone hanging around outside of my office...what can you tell me about this person?"

"He was about five-feet-six-inches in height,

he had long brown hair and a small moustache, he wore green jeans, a pink T-shirt and white trainers. He wore a cross around his neck and a skull-shaped ring on his left little finger."

"That is excellent Paul. What wonderful powers of observation and recall you have! Can you tell me anything about this person's frame of mind?"

"Urm...he was in a hurry?"

"He certainly was, and he also looked very angry...because I told him to look angry!" Paul and Joe looked at Zeigarnik with puzzlement on their faces. "I have a little confession to make...that man was a stooge. He is my research assistant whom I'd instructed early this morning to make an appearance at 2.30 outside my office and to act the part of an angry and frustrated man who had an urgent errand. It is the perfect test...to see whether Paul could remember details of an unexpected encounter!" Joe Bertolli shook his head in disbelief as Paul continued to look bemused.

-Chapter 8-

Getting Knotted

As arranged, on the following Saturday, Joe Bertolli jumped into his Ford Capri and drove to Paul's house, where he found Paul awaiting him anxiously by the front door. They had arranged to meet Dr Benjamin Zeigarnik at Greenwich Police Station at 10.00 and it was already 09.55.

"Hi Paul! Sorry I'm late...think I need a new car. Took me ages to get this heap started. So, are you ready for our visit to the station?" Paul nodded at Joe and quickly jumped into the passenger seat in the front of the car. Joe then briefed Paul about their imminent meeting with Dr Zeigarnik. When the three were together in Zeigarnik's office last Monday, they had agreed to meet at Greenwich

71

Police Station today to try to generate some new ideas about Mr Sheen. "So Paul, we need to tackle this very knotty problem...or unknot all the knots, is the way I'm thinking about it. We have a lot of evidence about a number of very unusual burglaries and it all points to a serial offender. We don't know why he does what he does...or more precisely, we don't know why he does it the *way* he does it. What is clear is that these burglaries have been taking place for years and are likely to continue unless we stop him." Paul gazed thoughtfully at Joe and nodded his head slowly in agreement.

When they reached the station, Joe saw Benjamin Zeigarnik perched on a metallic-red Lambretta scooter and in the midst of a lively discussion with two uniformed policemen. Joe Bertolli strode over to the policemen and said "It's OK, he's with me."

"It's OK Sarge, we're just admiring the

Lambretta. My old man used to have one and PC Wing here used to ride motorbikes in his youth. Beautiful machine, this."

Joe motioned to Paul to join him and Zeigarnik at the entrance to the station. They ascended the stairs to the third floor where Joe led them to one of the interview rooms. "Can I get anyone a drink?"

"A strong black coffee for me please...and not any rubbish from the drinks vending machine!" demanded Benjamin. Bertolli made daggers with his eyes as he stared at Zeigarnik in irritation.

"Um...can I have a Coke please?" Paul's request was almost apologetic, as though such frills would be inappropriate in a police station. "Of course you can Paul. I'll be right back."

Joe returned hot-foot with the drinks and handed them over. Zeigarnik stared at his polystyrene cup with raised eyebrows and a pained expression on his face.

"Now to business! Thanks to both of you for making time on a weekend to come to the station. As I mentioned before, I'd like both of you here with your very different perspectives so that we can try to unravel the mystery that is Mr Sheen. Three heads are better than one and I hope that by the end of this morning, I'll have some concrete ideas to present to my colleagues. Our investigation needs an injection of new ideas as we have reached a total dead-end with our approaches so far. As a starting point, let's each take a turn to speculate about Mr Sheen's motives...Benjamin?"

"I think Mr Sheen is driven by some kind of mental pathology that arose from some loss in his childhood...possibly the death of a parent. I would guess that his childhood was up to that point a fairly happy one and spent in quite a fine house, as he seems to be targeting large, expensive houses. He ransacks everything in these houses not so much for financial gain, but as trophies...trophies of a cosy childhood."

"OK Benjamin, thanks for that idea. As Paul is the only one to have seen Mr Sheen, let's see if there's anything that Paul remembers about his appearance; something that might tell us a bit about his state of mind." Joe swept his gaze to Paul's face and gently asked him if he could remember anything relevant, to which Paul replied that Mr Sheen looked very ordinary. Joe's thoughts returned to Benjamin Zeigarnik's hypothesis. "If Benjamin is right and we are dealing with a nostalgic trophy hunter, then I would expect to see a bit more selectivity in what he steals from these houses...and why the obsessive cleaning of each property? Paul, what do you think drives our burglar?"

Paul looked into the middle distance as he

tried to marshal his thoughts. "I think that maybe Mr Sheen is looking for something and he hasn't found it yet because if he had, he wouldn't carry on breaking into houses and cleaning them. If he gathers all the dust in the house, he must be looking for something very small. Something small that is to be found in large houses. So I'm thinking he's looking for something that can barely be seen by the human eye and could easily be missed if lying on the floor or on a table. Then I started thinking about all the things that would show up on a duster when we wipe a table or floor: dust, powders, bits of food, liquids, hair. Then I started thinking about something I heard in one of my Biology classes: that forensic scientists can sometimes extract DNA from dust as it sometimes contains dead skin cells...and of course hair is also used for DNA analysis. So maybe Mr Sheen is searching for someone and is ransacking these houses in order to collect DNA

76

samples to identify them...or maybe he just has mental problems like Dr Zeigarnik says?"

Both Zeigarnik and Bertolli were speechless. The psychologist's mind was trapped in a recurring loop, cycling between total conviction in the boy's genius and dismay at the earnest infantile yarn-spinning. The sergeant was just flabbergasted by the compelling conclusion reached by the youngster's highly analytical mind.

Bertolli was the first to break the stifling silence. "Joe, that was very impressive. I wonder why Mr Sheen is focusing only on large, expensive houses? Could it be that he's looking for a particular individual who happens to be rich? Or is he trying to find a former partner-in- crime who became rich from his past crimes?"

Zeigarnik let out a whistle of surprise, took a deep and loud breath, squared his shoulders and looked in turn at Paul and Joe. "Well...I don't know whether Paul's analysis is valid, but I grant you that the young man has a fine, imaginative mind. If you are right Paul, then Mr Sheen must have started with a sample of DNA from the identified individual, so that a comparison can be made with any DNA that he finds in the houses he burgles. So, Mr Sheen is either a molecular biologist of some kind who can do his own DNA analysis, or he knows one who does it for him."

Joe Bertolli became very excited by Zeigranik's speculation. "Benjamin, I think with Paul's help, you may have struck gold. We need to find a DNA analyst who offers his services to the public and who has been asked to analyse DNA samples by a person matching Mr Sheen's description. We would also expect that this customer has employed the services of the DNA analyst on a number of occasions and on dates corresponding roughly to the dates of the burglaries! I'll speak to my boss about this and see if she'll approve an investigation into DNA analysts in London."

By the time the three collaborators exited through the double-swing doors of the police station and entered the car park, Bertolli was beginning to entertain doubts about the direction that their speculations had taken. He couldn't fully convince himself that they had uncovered Mr Sheen's motives and it would be ten times as difficult to convince Chief Inspector Gravesham and the rest of his colleagues that they were on the right track...but that would have to wait for another day. He took Paul home and then drove to his own place and spent the rest of the day with his head buried in a long-neglected book on child psychology.

-Chapter 9-

Chief Reasons

Joe Bertolli's deep sleep was brought to an abrupt end by the incessant chimes of his ringtone. *Ahh, I need to change that cursed ringtone*, he vaguely thought to himself. Bleary eyed, he reached out for the 'phone and before he knew it, he was fumbling for it on the floor, where it had landed after coming into contact with a stray corner of his duvet. "Hello, Joe Bertolli here. Who is it?"

"Hi Joe, it's Mike. Sorry to wake you so early, but the boss is in a right state and wants you here pronto."

"Oh God, what time is it?" asked a very weary Bertolli, who loathed Monday mornings, especially when they started this early.

"It's 05.30 and you'd better get here at the station by 6.00, otherwise Gravesham will do her nut."

"Okay, I'll be there!" Joe knew that Mike Chandler was smirking with glee knowing that he'd disturbed his sleep and also put him on the spot. Mike wasn't such a bad cop, but like several colleagues at the station, had allowed himself to be drafted in by the Evil One as a passive tormentor of Joe Bertolli. He couldn't quite remember when he had first started thinking of Chief Inspector Gravesham as the "Evil One"; there was a time when they got along quite well. It probably all went wrong shortly after Joe's wife filed for divorce and he lost his home and other creature comforts. Selling his respectable Ford Mondeo and replacing it with the old, beat-up Ford Capri probably hadn't endeared him to her either. As for the rest of his colleagues, they seemed to resent his previous successes in solving crimes, as well as his independent cast of mind and quirky personality. He has to admit to himself that he was not a typical cop. In fact, he only got along with one colleague, apart from the psychologist Dr Benjamin Zeigarnik and that was Detective Maxine Carter. Maxine was a Maths whizz who had graduated from University College London only a few years ago. As much as she loved numbers, Maxine decided that she needed a life of action and applied to Hendon Police Academy the year after she'd left university. At Hendon, she was the top cadet, excelling in all the academic and physical disciplines on the curriculum. Maxine was now the station's main number-cruncher and computer geek, who spent hours most days looking for meaningful patterns in various data sets. Colleagues at Greenwich Police Station perceived Maxine Carter as only slightly more normal than Joe Bertolli.

The white Capri screeched to a juddering halt at the entrance-gate to the police station and Joe Bertolli sprang up the twelve steps to the double-doors of the building. Running along the corridor to the detectives' meeting room he stole a glance at the clock on the far-side wall before veering left to the room where his waiting colleagues had assembled. Damn, six minutes late! As Joe entered, the background chatter had turned to silence as his good morning greeting was met by one or two icy stares and a couple of smirks. "You're late!" announced the booming voice of Detective Chief Inspector Sara Gravesham, as she turned her back to him and strode to the whiteboard. Three of the four police officers present quickly assumed their seats and faced DCI Gravesham. Maxine Carter hesitated and waited for Joe to approach a chair and then chose a seat close to him.

DCI Gravesham picked up a blue marker-pen

and very slowly wrote a word at the top of the white-board: BRAINSTORM. She then turned quickly and stared directly into Joe Bertolli's bleary eyes. "Contrary to all that is just and proper, some of us are blessed with gifts and abilities beyond what we deserve. YOU Sergeant Bertolli are one such individual. As much as it pains me to say this, your fervid brain often produces helpful speculations that lead to solutions of the most complicated cases. But before you get too pleased with yourself, I would thank you to remember that crime-solving is a team sport that depends just as much on Chandler here as it does on you. Please get the ball rolling!"

Bertolli broke the stunned silence in the meeting room by clearing his throat. He then got up from his seat and sauntered to the whiteboard. "Hm, hm...thank you Chief. Well, I think we need to start by thinking hard...er, brainstorming...about Mr

Sheen's MO. Why does he target large houses, loot them, and then return at a later time or date to give the place a deep-clean?" Joe decided that it would be a bad idea to offer Paul Kanner and Benjamin Zeigarnik's ideas to the assembled detectives, as they would dismiss these out of hand. Maybe it would be best to see if the other detectives came up with plausible ideas.

"Maybe he is insane" offered Mike Chandler.

"He is too careful and organised to be insane" retorted Bertolli.

"Maybe he wants to ensure he hasn't left any clues, such as DNA from any of his fallen hairs" offered Modi Urghar, another officer who did not particularly like Bertolli.

"But why come back later to do this: it increases his risk of being seen and getting caught" replied Bertolli.

"He comes back later to make sure all

airborne clues have settled down to the floor before he bothers to clean up" stated Maxine Carter with a twinkle in her eye and a faint smile. "That way, DNA from loose hairs and dandruff and so on can be picked up" she continued. Joe Bertolli went into a trance as he considered Maxine's idea. There was something intriguing about it that felt right, but also, something that didn't quite add up. Before Bertolli could reply, DCI Gravesham beat him to it and uttered what had finally dawned on him.

"But that makes no sense at all. Our criminal, whom you insist on calling Mr Sheen, must surely know that it would be a logistic nightmare for us to work out whether the DNA belonged to him or to the occupants of the household. Why go to so much trouble?"

The penny finally dropped! The great light-bulb moment had finally occurred. Sgt Joe Bertolli's face broke out into a beaming smile as he peered at

DCI Gravesham. He now felt confident that he could spring Paul and Benjamin's ideas onto these detectives. "Of course! He's not trying to eliminate clues to his own identity...he's trying to find someone else's identity! He's not trying to clear away particles containing his own DNA, he's trying to *collect* DNA!"

His triumphant smile froze on his face as DCI Gravesham calmly gazed at him and asked the obvious question: "Why? Why would he want to know *who* the occupants of the house are...surely, he could look this up in a directory?" Paul looked down at his feet and decided not to elaborate further on the ideas that Paul and Benjamin had generated until they could find ways of testing these. Hopefully, he could buy a bit of time so that he could meet for another session with Paul and Benjamin.

DCI Gravesham brought the meeting to a

close having reluctantly acknowledged that perhaps some kind of progress had been made in working out Mr Sheen's motives. "It pains me to say this, but there probably is something in Sgt Bertolli's suggestion, as all the other ideas just don't add up. I suggest that Sgt Bertolli continues with his line of inquiry and reports back to me early next week."

-Chapter 10-

Messages

The white Capri screeched to a halt outside 29 Bertram Street and Joe Bertolli beeped the car horn even before the car had juddered to a stop. Mr Kanner opened the front door and waved to Joe, simultaneously shouting for Paul to come down.

"Hey Paul, jump in. We're running a bit late for our appointment with Benjamin at his University of London hideaway. How have you been?" Paul's expressionless face peered at Joe Bertolli's neck as though his muscles lacked the energy to take his gaze all the way up to Bertolli's face. It wasn't that Paul was displeased to see Joe Bertolli...in fact, he'd been looking forward to doing a bit more detective work with the sergeant. Paul felt as though he was withering under all the scrutiny he was receiving...from his frantic parents, his over-expectant teachers and some of his more brainless peers.

"Paul, I have some great news! DCI Sara Gravesham bought your idea that Mr Sheen might be trying to collect someone's DNA when he's doing his deep-clean. So, when we meet up with Benjamin, we can explore the other idea you two geniuses came up with, and concentrate on the messages left by Mr Sheen on the walls of the houses he has burgled." Paul's mood lifted when he heard this and he summoned the energy to raise his gaze all the way to Bertolli's face and even managed a weak smile.

Bertolli's white Capri pulled up at the gates of the University of London's Senate House. Within seconds, an agitated security guard started shouting and gesticulating in the general direction of Joe

Bertolli. The sergeant put on his menacing sunglasses, got out of his car, and slammed shut the driver's door. He found the security guard right in front of him jabbing his forefinger towards his chest. Bertolli produced his warrant card, smiled wryly at the security guard and beckoned Paul to follow him.

"Hope you're feeling fit Paul. My feet still hurt from climbing all those stairs last time we were here. Let's hope Benjamin has ordered in some decent snacks and coffee...oh, and Coke." As they clambered up the interminable steps, Bertolli noticed that Paul had an increasingly far-away look and expressed his concern.

"I'm okay", replied Paul. "Just thinking-erm...about the case of Mr Sheen." Bertolli felt a measure of relief to hear this, as he had wondered whether Paul was ruminating about personal problems with family and school. Just another two flights of steps to go!

Finally, Joe and Paul arrived at the landing with the signpost to Benjamin Zeigarnik's lab and offices. They stood in front of the closed door which reminded Paul of something out of an old private detective movie. The door was made of steel and had frosted glass in the top half, with distinctive lettering: **C07.15 Forensic Psychology Laboratory: Dr Benjamin Zeigarnik**. Just as Joe Bertolli raised his arm to knock, the door swung open and Benjamin Zeigarnik appeared with a flourish.

"Hello my friends! Good to see you. Paul, I'm so glad that you brought along your assistant, Sergeant Joe Bertolli. Let us hope he will be of assistance to us on this occasion!" Paul smiled uncertainly as Joe shot through the gap between Benjamin and the door. Paul followed Bertolli into Zeigarnik's lab, where his attention was drawn to the array of computer screens and other gizmos on display.

"I'm sure your mother told you how funny you were as a little boy Benjamin. This might explain why you try so hard and achieve so little". Bertolli's barbed remark had Zeigarnik doubling up with laughter, which of course was not the intended outcome. "Okay, let's get down to it! The good news Benjamin is that Gravesham is taking seriously the idea that our Mr Sheen might be cleaning up in order to collect someone else's DNA...someone that he has spent many years looking for. The big question is who is this person?"

Zeigarnik raised his eyebrows in mock surprise before adding "Another big question is what does he want to do when he has found this person?" Both Joe and Paul narrowed their eyes in concentration as they contemplated the enormity of the task ahead of them.

Zeigarnik continued: "If I recall correctly, the

purpose of today's little get-together is to consider the messages that Mr Sheen has left on the walls of the houses he has burgled. I have copied all of these into my notebook, which I shall pass round in a minute. All of these messages seem to boil down to three central themes: 1) something that is rightfully his was taken away from him; 2) he wants this back; 3) he wants revenge for his loss." As he passed his notebook to Paul, he continued with his analysis. "My guess is that a former partner-in-crime took off without giving Mr Sheen his agreed share of the ill-gotten gains. One might further speculate that this partner snitched on him and he ended up in prison. So, he wants to have his fair share of the money back, or whatever it was that they stole and revenge for being stitched up. So, he's dusting houses to see if there's a match with a sample of his former partner's DNA that he has already had analysed by one of these commercial DNA analysis companies. "

Zeigarnik smiled broadly, obviously pleased with the lucidity and inescapable certainty of his analysis, as Bertolli examined the notebook. Paul mumbled something and looked at the floor. "Paul, I didn't catch what you were saying" Zeigarnik stated in a gentle way.

"Oh...I said...um...'it was never his'...so he can't be trying to get something back that he never had in the first place." Paul blushed crimson in anticipation of an annoyed outburst from Zeigarnik. Bertolli looked at them both, wondering how this situation would resolve itself. Suddenly, Zeigarnik burst into laughter and playfully slapped Paul on the back.

"My very clever friend" he said as he realised that perhaps it was time to stop slapping Paul's back. "Yes, you have a very good point there. Maybe someone stole something from *him*, and he wants *that* back!"

Bertolli shook his head and decided to offer his own interpretation of the messages. "Hold on a second. One of the things that strikes me about some of the messages is that they are kind of emotional, as though he is deeply attached to what has been taken away from him...like a person! Maybe someone he loved was taken away from him...and who is usually taken away from an adult? Maybe a child? Maybe his child was taken into care because of Mr Sheen's criminal activities, or maybe his wife disappeared with their child to get away from him."

Zeigarnik looked first at Bertolli, then at Paul. "Well, well my friends. If you're right, then we have to assume that the owners of the houses he burgles are very significant. He must be targeting houses owned by people that he thinks are connected in some way to his missing child or whoever it is that he's looking for."

Joe Bertolli smiled broadly. He felt relieved that the solution to the Mr Sheen case might finally rest on routine police procedures. The next step would be to locate and contact the owners of the most recent houses burgled by Mr Sheen and see what could be uncovered about their family history.

-Chapter 11-

In Search of Lost Ties

Sgt Joe Bertolli sat at the edge of the swivel chair, his face a picture of total concentration as he stared at his desktop screen. The station was quieter than usual and he was glad that he had decided to come in this Sunday evening. Barely five hours had elapsed since his meeting with Paul and Benjamin and he was raring to go. He knew that the next step was to identify the owners of the houses burgled by Mr Sheen and unearth any common threads that potentially linked them together. To keep things manageable, Bertolli decided that in the first instance, he would only focus on the ten most recent houses that had been burgled in the peculiar way suggestive of Mr Sheen's handiwork.

98

As the Metropolitan Police Primary Data Base loaded up on the screen, Joe Bertolli hurriedly thought up some key words that would help him conduct his search: he typed in **burglary; large house; empty house; cleaned**. He was then presented with questions about the information he required: he typed in: **owner's name; owner's personal details; names of family members; family members' personal details**. In response to number of records to extract, he typed: **most recent 10**. In twenty seconds, the computer produced the results he was looking for in ten neat paragraphs.

A quick scan of the ten records brought a smile to Joe Bertolli's lips. The owners of the ten burgled houses had very similar surnames: **(1) McDonald; (2) MacDougall; (3) McDriscoll; (4) McNaught; (5) McGarrigle; (6) McVey; (7) MacDonald; (8) MacKenzie; (9) McDonnell; (10) McKay**. It would appear that Mr Sheen was looking for someone specific after all. Interestingly, most of the house-owners were quite elderly, lived abroad and rented their house out from time to time. This would explain why Mr Sheen targeted empty houses. The personal details of all ten house-owners suggested that they were quite wealthy. Seven of the ten had been married and had grown-up children, and in two cases, there was a step-child in the household. This gave Bertolli an idea: if Mr Sheen is looking for a child that had in some way been taken away from him, then maybe the child had been adopted by one of these characters.

Focusing on the two records that mentioned a step-child, Joe Bertolli tried to make sense of the information contained in the records:-

Record 7: House-owner: John MacDonald

Personal details: 78 year of age; retired investment banker; married to Laura Cummings (55) on August 2nd, 1972, (divorced on January 21st, 1996) and Helen Maxwell (43) on August 3rd, 2010; three children: Mary (45); Paul (34); David (13), step-child; normally resident in Thessaloniki, Greece.

Record 9: House-owner: Jack McDonnell

Personal details: 73 years of age; retired businessman; married to Margaret Hughes (38), July 15th, 2010; one child: Peter (14), step-child; normally resident in Santander, Spain.

Joe Bertolli scratched his head and wondered whether either the thirteen-year-old David MacDonald or the fourteen-year-old Peter McDonnell was the biological son of the man that the press and police called Mr Sheen. The ages fit: the Mr Sheen burglaries started about twelve years ago. If he could check the marriage records, he should be able to find out whether the two mothers, Helen Maxwell and Margaret Hughes had been married before. Joe Bertolli called up the website for Births, Deaths and Marriages, and entered the two women's names in the search box. He found numerous entries for both Helen Maxwell and Margaret Hughes. Unfortunately, it seemed that the two women had never married before, so the records could not be used as leads to the identity of Mr Sheen. He also checked the birth records of David MacDonald and Peter McDonnell, which should indicate the name of their father. Curiously, in both cases, the entry for father's name read **unknown**. It would seem that he wasn't going to get his answer from the public records after all. He would have to find a way of interviewing the two women in the hope that they led him to Mr Sheen. He guessed that one or both of these women might be harbouring a secret about the identity of their child's father and getting at the truth would be far from straightforward. He would have to consult his friend Dr Benjamin Zeigarnik for some expert advice.

-Chapter 12-

Questions and Answers

Before leaving the station Joe Bertolli used his office 'phone to call Benjamin Zeigarnik, who answered after a single ring. Joe explained the latest developments in the Mr Sheen case and then asked Benjamin when he could come to see him to discuss how to proceed with interviewing Mrs MacDonald and Mrs McDonnell. "I am truly very sorry Joe, but I am up to my eyes in work and won't be able to spare you a single minute for the next four days. Let us quickly discuss the matter now on the 'phone."

The 'quick discussion' went on for almost an hour, as Dr Benjamin Zeigarnik liked nothing better than giving people advice. He suggested that Joe should not reveal his true purpose when

104

questioning the two women; if one of them had been the partner of Mr Sheen, they are bound to be secretive about this. It would be better to use the actual burglaries as a pretext for arranging to meet them. Zeigarnik also advised Bertolli to be on the look-out for deception when the two women answered any questions to do with their young son or his biological father. In his inimitable words, Zeigarnik stated rather forcefully "Joe, *listen* for the lies, don't *look* for the lies. When people lie about a topic, they hesitate more and give you much less detail than when they're being truthful about something. Don't waste your time looking at their body language...this can mislead you! It might help to close your eyes when you're interviewing them so that you're not distracted by their fake facial expressions and so on. As my colleague Professor Wiseman once said..."

"Whoa, hold on Benjamin! This is getting very

confusing. Are you seriously expecting me to stand there, notebook in hand, interviewing each woman with my eyes closed? That would give them every reason to be suspicious of my intentions and I would feel..."

"OK, I was only joking about closing your eyes! I just wanted to make a point here. You know, it might be best to conduct an initial interview over the 'phone so that you can concentrate on their answers. I also advise that you take young Paul with you when you do interview them in person at their home. Paul might be able to get some relevant information from the kids themselves. It would also be useful if Paul managed to get some hair from the two kids so that we can analyse their DNA. If one of them is related to Mr Sheen, and Mr Sheen has a criminal record, we should be able to match the kid's DNA sample with what is on the Crime Base DNA Register to find out who Mr Sheen is."

"Thank you Benjamin, I always said you were brilliant. I will call Mrs MacDonald and Mrs McDonnell right away."

Joe Bertolli was relieved to be able to reach both Mrs MacDonald and Mrs McDonnell on their landline 'phones. Thankfully, they were in their London homes where he could easily interview them. His pretext for calling and requesting an interview was that the Metropolitan Police were following up all of the open cases of burglary that had occurred within the past seven years. He explained that he was in charge of this operation and that he hoped that this would throw new light on what the police now realised was a series of linked crimes. Both women seemed hesitant in responding to his questions, which reminded Bertolli to follow Dr Zeigarnik's advice on spotting lies.

Early the following evening, Bertolli found

107

himself at the front door of Helen and John MacDonald, with the young Paul Kanner in tow. He rang the doorbell and was greeted by a cautious "Yes, who...is it?" through the small opening of the door. Bertolli detected a slight tremor in Mrs MacDonald's voice. "Hello Mrs MacDonald, it's Sgt Joe Bertolli of the Metropolitan Police. I have an appointment to speak to you about your burglary." The door opened to reveal a flustered Helen MacDonald whose face and neck were bright crimson. She looked as though she was about to burst into tears.

Bertolli shook Mrs MacDonald's hand and introduced Paul as a friend's son that he was looking after. "So sorry, it was all very last minute. I'm sure Paul won't bother us. Is there anyone else in the house he can talk to while we're conducting the interview? Or maybe he can just sit quietly in your kitchen?" Mrs MacDonald gave Paul an appraising look and mentioned that her husband was away on business, but her son David was around. She called David's name and a teenage boy with long dark hair and a thin frame appeared within seconds.

While Paul and David busied themselves with a game of *Assassin's Creed*, Bertolli gently probed Mrs MacDonald for information about her son and his biological father, but was met with hesitant and vague answers. She said that David's father was not listed on his birth certificate because her own parents disapproved of him. After repeated questioning, Mrs MacDonald revealed the identity of her son David's father. David's father was called Michael Chisholm. Michael had worked as an accountant when Mrs MacDonald used to go out with him. Her parents disapproved of him because he was frequently drunk and abusive. Her parents spirited her and the newborn David away, renting a flat for them in a different part of London. Soon afterwards, she had met John MacDonald, who seemed a steady and warm person who showed a heartfelt interest in David. They married when David was three and split their time between John's large London house and a small villa that they rented in Thessaloniki in Greece. She had not heard from Michael since David's birth, but then again, she'd had to be secretive about her whereabouts, only letting a few select friends in on the secret.

Joe Bertolli was captivated by Mrs Helen MacDonald's account and felt a rising sense of excitement that Michael Chisholm may well be their man: Mr Sheen finally exposed! He had one more question to ask before he went on his way. "Mrs MacDonald, can you please tell me how Michael Chisholm felt about your pregnancy and about having a baby?"

Helen MacDonald looked directly at Bertolli and replied in a bitter voice: "He hated the whole thing. He kept saying that we shouldn't be having a baby...it would ruin his plans for a carefree life. He kept blaming me for the pregnancy...you'd think from the things he said that he had nothing to do with it! Anyway, David is a lovely son and John and I love him dearly, so he's the good thing that came out of a bad situation."

Joe Bertolli could not hide his feelings when Mrs MacDonald had concluded her account. He was crestfallen. He wished he hadn't asked such an obvious question. On the basis of what she'd said, it would seem extremely unlikely that Michael Chisholm was the mysterious Mr Sheen. He did not sound like a man who went through so much trouble to uncover the whereabouts of a long-lost son...unless of course, his attitude to being a father had radically changed in the intervening years.

Bertolli half-heartedly called Paul as he thanked Mrs MacDonald for her time and assured her that the Metropolitan Police were working overtime on catching the burglar and retrieving her stolen possessions.

Bertolli opened the front passenger door for Paul, then lumbered over to the driver's side of the car, opened the door and slumped heavily into his seat. He held his head in his hands and rubbed his eyes with his palms in a way that suggested that he wanted to erase what was going on behind them in his brain. Paul was oblivious to all this as he triumphantly held up a matted clump of dark fibres reminiscent of a home-knitted rug. "I've got them!" he exclaimed. "David is even more untidy than me...my mum would throw him out of the window if he lived in our house. Socks, bits of hair and other rubbish lying all over the place! I bet we've got plenty of material here to extract his DNA." Bertolli reconfigured his face into a less than convincing smile before firing up the engine of his Capri.

Their next stop was the house of Margaret and Jack McDonnell. Mr McDonnell opened the door and gazed appraisingly at Bertolli and his young sidekick. Bertolli made the introductions as he was beckoned into the house. When Bertolli explained Paul's presence Mr McDonnell said it was a pity that his son Peter was visiting his grandparents in Wandsworth, otherwise he'd love to challenge Paul to a game of *Call of Duty*. Mrs McDonnell hovered aimlessly just as Bertolli and Paul entered the hallway behind Mr McDonnell. Bertolli sensed a certain tension in the couple and wondered why they were more nervous than other people who had to face questioning from the police. When he and Paul were guided to the sitting room he put the married couple at their ease by commenting on how beautiful their furnishings

113

were. He then went on to explain that the purpose of his visit was to try to unearth more clues as the Metropolitan Police force now suspected that they were dealing with a serial offender. After routine questioning, Bertolli broached the subject of young Peter.

"One line of enquiry that we're pursuing is that the burglar may be committing these peculiar crimes as a way of punishing the house-owners. I wonder if either of you can tell me anything about people known to you that might fit this theory." Mr and Mrs McDonnell looked at each other conspiratorially and then shook their heads.

Jack McDonnell broke the silence. "No Sergeant. I hate to disappoint you but our lives are perfectly boring and orderly and there are no skeletons in our closets. Everyone that we know is in gainful employment and has neither the time nor the inclination to go round burgling and cleaning houses!"

Bertolli's instincts were telling him that he was not going to get much information from this couple...and he was beginning to wonder whether their son Peter's absence was strategic rather than coincidental. Maybe they feared that the boy might let something slip in some way that would raise the policeman's suspicions. In any event, he had to be very careful with his next question as he did not want to cause offence, which would lead to the McDonnell's clamming up completely. "Mrs McDonnell, could I ask *you* a question before I leave? I can see that you and Mr McDonnell have built a fantastic life for yourselves and Peter and it's obvious to me that you have put a lot of thought and hard work into creating such a lovely home. Please don't take this the wrong way, but I do need to eliminate from our enquiries one key person from your past. What can you tell me about Peter's biological father?"

Mrs McDonnell was clearly startled by Bertolli's question and gazed at him uncomprehendingly. "Erm...sorry, you've caught me by surprise. Well, what can I tell you? I hadn't known him for very long...er, he was some kind of artist. He didn't know about Peter...erm...we broke up early in my pregnancy. He didn't know I was pregnant. One day, out of the blue, he called to say that he didn't think it was going to work out between us. Thankfully, I haven't heard from him since."

Bertolli softened his gaze as he could tell Mrs McDonnell was distressed by her recollections of this unhappy episode in her past. He also sensed that she was hiding something from him, this impression being reinforced by her and her husband's downcast eyes. If Mrs McDonnell was telling the truth, it would seem that Peter's biological father was an unlikely candidate for Mr Sheen. He thanked the couple for their time and said he'd be in touch with any new developments. Paul was already waiting by the front door when Mr McDonnell came to let them out.

It was eerily silent in the car as Bertolli turned the ignition key. Nothing happened. After repeated attempts, the engine coughed and spluttered as a plume of black smoke made its way out of the car's exhaust pipe. Juddering out of the driveway and onto the road, the car stalled momentarily and then restarted with an explosive sound. Bertolli let out a loud stress-busting laugh as he turned to look at Paul. "Nice cap you've got there Paul...hadn't noticed it before. New is it?"

"It's not really mine. I sort of...stole it. It belongs to that kid Peter McDonnell. I saw it on the floor near the coat hooks and thought we could use it...might be some hairs and dandruff and stuff that contains his DNA". Bertolli looked at Paul and smiled genuinely for the first time all day.

-Chapter 13-

Testing···Testing

The following morning, a dispirited Joe Bertolli arrived at Greenwich Police Station and immediately slumped into his office chair. After all the excitement generated by the missing-son hypothesis, he felt doubly deflated. His interviews with Mrs MacDonald and the McDonnells left him feeling that he was on the wrong trail. It seemed that both kids' biological fathers were disinterested, which ruled them out as candidates for Mr Sheen. But who knows, maybe he hadn't been told the truth about one of these men. Still, he had a large sample of David MacDonald's hair as well as a sample of hairs taken from Peter McDonnell's cap, so he might as well send those off to the Forensics Lab for analysis. He picked up the 'phone and made the necessary arrangements for the hair-samples to be sent for DNA analysis.

Nursing a steaming mug of strong black coffee, Bertolli engrossed himself in the task of reviewing the Mr Sheen case. What his thoughts kept returning to was the similarities in the surnames of the house-owners burgled by Mr Sheen. Surely, Mr Sheen was searching for *someone*, even if this person wasn't a long-lost son. Could Mr Sheen be trying to trace a partner-in-crime who had cheated on him in some way? But he had checked all of the home-owners and none had a criminal record.

Three long days passed and the DNA test results were still not ready. Feeling frustrated, Bertolli decided to call Dr Zeigarnik. "We need to meet up Benjamin. Do you have any time available?" Zeigarnik indicated that he would be free in a couple of days' time, on Saturday morning.

He also suggested that Paul Kanner should be present at the meeting. Bertolli filled him in on what he had learned from interviewing Helen MacDonald and the McDonnells, and that he was waiting for DNA profiles of the two hair samples. When he finished, he took a deep breath and tried to shut out the intrusive thought that the case of Mr Sheen had reached a dead-end.

On Saturday, Joe Bertolli picked Paul up from his home in Bertram Street and drove to Greenwich Police Station where they were due to meet Benjamin Zeigarnik. As Joe entered the car-park he could see a gleaming red Lambretta scooter and leaning on it, a smiling Benjamin Zeigarnik, with arms folded, oozing self-satisfaction.

"Ah, Joe...Paul...at last, you decided to join me! I need a coffee and fast!"

Bertolli gave Benjamin a withering look and coolly told him to follow him as he strode to the entrance of the police station. Once inside, Bertolli brought everyone their favoured drinks and sat heavily on his swivel chair as he beckoned the other two to sit. "I'm still waiting on the results of the DNA profiles for those two boys. I think it will probably be a waste of time anyway, as it looks as though their biological fathers do not fit the bill.

Zeigarnik shook his head in sympathy. "Joe my friend, this case is becoming more and more complex. Maybe we're going to have to be patient and flexible...explore different avenues." Bertolli rubbed his face as he tried to think of a new "avenue" to explore. He was now convinced more than ever that he was being stitched up by DCI Sara Gravesham in order to be publicly humiliated by his failure to identify and catch Mr Sheen. Zeigarnik shifted his focus to the very silent boy next to him and noticed that Paul's brows were distinctly knitted and he looked both puzzled and very worried.

"Paul, my cleverer friend, how are you? You know, Joe and I need to say a big "thank you" to you for all that you've contributed to this case. Is there something that you'd like to say?"

Paul gazed ahead and seemed lost for words for some seconds. Finally, he summoned up the courage to ask the question that had been plaguing him for several days. "Well, I was thinking...the DNA samples from the two boys...they're from houses that Mr Sheen burgled quite a long time ago. If they matched what he was looking for, why is he carrying on burgling houses? So Mr Sheen must *know* that they don't match the DNA of his son...so this means we won't be able to find out who Mr Sheen is through the DNA analysis of David and Peter's hair."

Zeigarnik and Bertolli simultaneously arched their eyebrows and their eyes locked in mutual embarrassment. Zeigarnik broke the silence. "Well done Paul, you are absolutely correct...you have a very fine mind my friend. It is possible of course that Mr Sheen wasn't as lucky as you and Joe in finding good samples of the boys' DNA...so it is still possible that we may still strike gold." Joe Bertolli's face momentarily brightened while Paul continued to look worried. Zeigarnik decided to diffuse the tension in the room by giving Paul a mini-lesson on DNA profiling.

"Now Paul, I don't know how much you already know about DNA profiling, but let me tell you a little bit about how it will be done in this case. First, we need a clean and sizeable sample of a person's cells. The nucleus of these cells contains the DNA that will be extracted for analysis. Hair found on the floor is sometimes not a good source material because the DNA becomes damaged with time when it is not in a living person's scalp. We have to hope that the DNA technician was able to extract enough DNA from these hair cells. Once this is done, the technician will analyse 16 specific sections of DNA. These 16 sections are analysed for what are called Short Tandem Repeats. Different people have different numbers of repeats of a pattern. These 16 numbers are called a DNA profile. We can use these to compare each boy's DNA profiles to profiles on the National DNA Database. Hopefully, the DNA profile of one of the boys will closely match the DNA profile of a criminal...we'll then know the true identity of Mr Sheen."

Before Paul could fully process what Zeigarnik had told him, his thoughts were interrupted by a very loud ringtone. Bertolli picked up his mobile 'phone. It was Dr Karl Leaburn calling from the DNA Profiling Section of the Forensic Lab to give Joe Bertolli the results: the DNA of the two boys did not match that of anyone on the National DNA

Database. Damn...a dead end! Bertolli thanked Dr Leaburn and immediately turned to Benjamin and Paul to inform them of the disappointing news.

-Chapter 14-

Loose Ends

Joe Bertolli and Paul Kanner drove in silence to Paul's house in Bertram Street. When Mrs Kanner opened the front door, Paul looked at Joe and gave him a weak smile. "Do you like to play darts Sergeant...I mean Joe?" With a nod of Bertolli's head as an answer, Paul led the way to the dartboard in the garage attached to the house. Mrs Kanner seemed very pleased...someone else could now put up with Paul for an hour or two.

After some practice-throws of the darts, Bertolli scratched his head and looked quizzically at Paul. "How do you feel Paul?" When his question was met with Paul's expressionless face, he continued to talk. "Benjamin was right you know...you have contributed a lot to this case and I am very grateful to you, no matter how the case goes. Still, it is frustrating as hell not being able to see a new way forward. I really was convinced that Mr Sheen was searching for his long-lost son. Maybe he is and hasn't found him yet. We would need to spend a long time tracking down people with 'Mac' or 'Mc' in their names, identifying those with large houses who leave them empty from time-to-time and then finding out about the owners' kids and then analysing more DNA samples...it all seems overwhelming and unwieldy. On top of this, we won't know whether these houses are on his target-list until *after* he has burgled them. I'd be spending the rest of my short career trying to keep up with him...and of course, we don't even know whether he has a criminal record, so we might not be able to match the DNA profiles in any case!"

Paul hit the bull's-eye with a dart and then

handed a dart to Bertolli. They played for twenty minutes or so before Paul uttered his first word. "I've been thinking. Erm...how does Mr Sheen choose the houses? If you knew you could guess which one was next and you could guard that house and maybe catch him." Paul looked awkwardly at the ground as Joe Bertolli tried to make sense of what he had just heard.

"So Paul, you're saying that Mr Sheen is systematically going through some kind of list of houses that might have what he's looking for? He's going through the list in some strict order...not keeping tabs on many houses at once and pouncing when one of these houses is empty?"

"Erm...I think so. That's the way I would do it...it's too hard watching over many houses. I would list all the houses in order and then focus on one at a time."

"Hmm...interesting Paul. Problem is, you

could be stuck for years waiting for the owners to vacate a particular house. Mind you, that might explain why he's spent years and years on these burglaries. It is really odd thinking about his targets: large houses with owners named 'Mac'-something or 'Mc'-something who spend quite a bit of time living away from home, presumably abroad. Who would be able to access and combine all this information and produce a list of houses to target? There are thousands of people in London with these surnames, so he couldn't have started by checking each one out...how would he find out if they had large houses and spent time away from home? He wouldn't be able to list every large house in London and then find out whether a 'Mac'-something or 'Mc'-something lived there and whether they spent time living away from home."

Paul raised his head and looked towards Bertolli with narrowed eyes. "It makes sense to start with people who regularly leave their house for long periods and then check names and addresses. You could then use Google Maps to find out whether it's a large house." Bertolli frowned and wondered why Mr Sheen would be targeting such highly specific properties. How would any person manage to collect all of the information necessary to compile a list of the sort that Paul had in mind?

Bertolli knew that they would not be solving the case of Mr Sheen any time soon. He thanked Paul for his help and the game of darts and broodily headed for his Ford Cortina, so engrossed in his thoughts that he forgot to bid farewell to Mrs Kanner.

-Chapter 15-

A Problem Shared

The following day, Joe Bertolli went unannounced to Dr Benjamin Zeigarnik's forensic psychology laboratory in Senate House. Benjamin swung open his office door, ready to bawl out the person who had interrupted him. When he saw a dejected Sgt Joe Bertolli, he silently opened the door as wide as it would go and beckoned him in.

"Joe, you look terrible! Not sleeping? This Mr Sheen case has got to you, hasn't it my friend?"

"Benjamin, I need your help. As you know, there are many burglaries in South-East London and I'm struggling to think of a way of anticipating future targets of Mr Sheen so that we can catch him. Do you have any new ideas?"

"Not really. I know that in the past you've had

police officers observe large houses burgled in case it's Mr Sheen and he makes a return, but he never does when there's a police presence, even though the police are out of sight. Whoever he is, Mr Sheen is a clever and cunning fox."

"I know! One time we had two plain-clothes police officers living for a whole week in a hotel across the street from one of the burgled houses. They gave up on the eighth day, and guess what? The very next day, a neighbour reported that they saw a man leaving the house in the middle of the night. When we entered the house, it became obvious that Mr Sheen had made one of his house-cleaning visits!"

"One suggestion for you Joe. Young Paul Kanner is very good at detecting patterns that you and I might miss. Have you shown him all the details of the previously burgled houses? Maybe he'll see a pattern in the order of the burglaries. You need to show him names of homeowners, addresses, and maybe a map with each burgled house pinpointed. You never know, if this Mr Sheen is as methodical as I think he is, he must be following a list of targets in a systematic order."

"Hah! That's more-or-less what Paul said when I last met him!"

Benjamin Zeigarnik smiled weakly as he escorted Joe Bertolli to the door. "Happy hunting Joe!"

Joe Bertolli jumped into his 'trusty' Ford Capri and drove southwards, entering a very congested Blackwall Tunnel, which took motorists across the River Thames. While the Capri crawled through the tunnel at a snail's pace, Bertolli planned the first order of business when he eventually returned to Greenwich Police Station.

Now at his desk, Bertolli called up the case file on Mr Sheen. He went through each burglary in sequence and then entered each of these on a map of South-East London. Bertolli looked at the printout and scratched his head. The first burglary took place almost eleven years ago in Deptford, the second burglary took place 6 miles away in Crystal Palace. The third burglary was in Woolwich, which was over 9 miles away from Crystal Palace. The latest burglary, which was Mr Sheen's 27th, was back in Crystal Palace. The sequence of burglaries seemed very random and it looked as though Mr Sheen was being opportunistic in his targets. Alternatively, he was going through an alphabetical list of homeowners' names and focusing on houses in that order.

Bertolli went back into the case file to check this. The first few burglaries showed that this hypothesis was also incorrect:-

1.	Deptford: Robert and Petra MacWhinney
2.	Crystal Palace: John and Mary McCarthy
3.	Woolwich: Jack MacIntyre
4.	Sydenham: John and Paula MacBeath
5.	Greenwich: Amy McCall

Joe Bertolli banged his desk in frustration and uttered a stream of choice swear- words. Detective Constable Maxine Carter watched the fuming Bertolli over her computer screen. "Is everything OK Joe? Do you need to talk?"

Bertolli got up and thrust the map in front of DC Carter. "Look at this incidents map. Can you see any systematic pattern in the order of these burglaries?"

Maxine Carter advised Bertolli to leave the

data with her: she could try out a new geographic profiling computer programme that she was developing. "It's still in the development stage, but maybe I'll be able to get something to you in a week or so."

Bertolli gave Maxine a wry smile and grabbed the printout of the map. He jumped into the Capri and was in Bertram Street in 5 minutes.

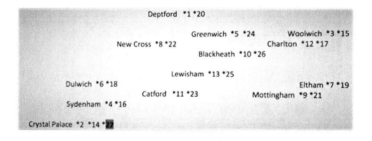

Mr Kanner called for Paul as soon as he saw Bertolli's haggard face. "Take a seat in the kitchen sergeant, Paul will be with you in a sec. I'll leave the two of you in peace to get on with your crime detection. Paul doesn't say much to us, so I don't know much about what this is all about. Maybe one day you'll tell me all about it. Can I get you a tea or coffee while you're waiting?"

Bertolli gave Mr Kanner a weak smile and politely refused his offer of a drink. "I'm sure that Paul will tell you all about this case once it's all over, but I'll be happy to fill you in on the details once we've concluded our inquiries." He had some misgivings about Mr Kanner and was desperately trying to stop his face and voice from betraying his thoughts. Admittedly, Paul was a teenager and had Asperger's Syndrome, but even so, his relationship with both his parents seemed much more strained than he'd imagined would normally be the case. He had read a bit about ASD in the child psychology book, which explained some of the challenges faced by parents, but even so, he felt Paul's parents were unnecessarily harsh and unappreciative of his strengths. His thoughts were interrupted by Paul's tentative entrance into the kitchen.

"Hi."

"Hi Paul, how are you?"

"Um...OK."

"Paul, I need to ask another favour of you. Here's a map with all of Mr Sheen's burglaries in sequence: the first was in Deptford, the second in Crystal Palace, the third in Woolwich and so on. As you can see, the latest one, which is the 27th that we know about, was back in Crystal Palace."

"Oh right...is that why it's shaded?"

"Yes, that's right Paul. What I'd like you to do is see whether there's a pattern in the sequence of burglaries. It seems random to me, but I thought you might be able to spot something that I've missed."

Paul narrowed his eyes and focused on the map. After a couple of minutes, he looked up with almost a grin. "After the first area he's chosen, he chooses the furthest place away from that one, then the furthest place again. When he's done all thirteen areas once, he chooses the furthest area away from the 13th as the 14th and then he carries on like this."

Bertolli looked puzzled for a minute or two before understanding the pattern that Paul had tried to describe. "Let me see. So he chose a house in Deptford as his first port of call; then he checked the map to see which is the furthest away for his second burglary and that happens to be...in Crystal Palace. Then he chose Woolwich, because it's further away from Crystal Palace than any of the other areas. When he's committed a burglary in each of the thirteen areas, he goes through a second round, again choosing on the basis of distance. It looks as though his latest burglary in Crystal Palace is the start of a third round. So he must be using telephone directories from these areas to find all the 'Mac'-something or 'Mc'-something surnames and then finding out which of them live in roads with large houses – maybe through Google Maps. So he must have a strong reason for believing that whatever he is looking for is in one of these areas of South-East London."

Paul gazed towards Bertolli and mumbled something that the distracted Bertolli failed to comprehend. "Sorry, what was that Paul?"

"Erm...his next burglary will be in Woolwich because that's the furthest away from Crystal Palace." Bertolli smiled for the first time in two weeks. The boy is a genius!

-Chapter 16-

Stake-Out

Thumbing through the telephone directory for the Woolwich area, Joe Bertolli came across thirteen candidate names and addresses. The one that struck him was the entry for Amy McNaught on Burrage Road. This road was well-known for its large houses, though many had been subdivided into flats in recent years. This particular house had not been subdivided and was owned in its entirety by Ms McNaught. Bertolli knew this because of the address: 821 Burrage Road. Houses that had been converted into flats had a house number followed by a letter specifying the flat, such as 182B. Bertolli grew quite excited because Mr Sheen's previous two burglaries in Woolwich had also taken place on Burrage Road. At last, he felt he was on the right track. He picked up his jacket and almost ran to the door of the big open-plan office that he shared with other detectives. As he opened the door, he saw that a grim-faced Detective Chief Inspector Sara Gravesham was marching straight towards him.

"It would seem that I have apprehended you just in the nick of time Sergeant Bertolli! I need to speak to you about the Mr Sheen case...I am sure you can spare me a moment." Sara Gravesham charged into the detectives' office following Bertolli's retreating figure. "I am very concerned by your lack of progress in this case and think now may be the time to hand over the reins to one of your colleagues." Bertolli raised both hands up in front of him as if trying to ward off any further threats to his self-esteem.

"Look, we've made a big breakthrough! We now understand how he selects properties to burgle, even though we don't fully understand why he cleans them up afterwards. I was just on my way to scope out what could be his next target." Bertolli explained how Paul Kanner and Benjamin Zeigarnik had helped him notice the patterning of the homeowners' names and the peculiarities of his geographical tactics. DCI Gravesham opened her mouth to reply to this latest news, but remaining silent, shook her head and briskly walked away. Bertolli let out a loud sigh of relief and ran out of the station, into the

car park and then climbed into his trusty Capri.

Five minutes had passed since DCI Gravesham's exit and Joe Bertolli was cruising cautiously along the length of Burrage Road. He saw 803 on the opposite side of the road and decided to park there and walk the remaining distance to 821. As he approached the house, he could see that the curtains were drawn in the upstairs and downstairs windows. Under different circumstances, it would strike a policeman as odd that all the curtains would be drawn at 11 a.m., but in this instance, Bertolli felt almost gleeful. 'This is it' he thought. 'The house must be empty...a perfect target for Mr Sheen!' He walked past the house to avert any suspicions and stopped at the street corner a few houses further along. He needed to think quickly about his next step. For all he knew, Mr Sheen could be in the vicinity right now. Bertolli decided to find out whether any of the neighbours knew when number 821 was vacated. It was an odd time of day to be knocking on people's doors as most people would be at work. Still, some people worked from home, so he might get lucky and find someone at home.

Bertolli strode up to the front door of 823 and grasped the ornate door-knocker, which was shaped like a lion's head and heaved it to make a series of three loud knocks. He felt very self-conscious as the road was very quiet and he was

145

convinced that Mr Sheen was prowling somewhere nearby. He furtively turned to look over his shoulder and then turned to face the front door again. He used the door-knocker again, hoping that this time, someone would answer and open the door. He waited for a minute before turning on his heels and strolling as casually as he could past 821 before turning into the driveway of 819. This door had a flimsy looking knocker that looked as though it would fly off so Bertolli rang the bell on the right-hand side of the door-frame. Rapid footsteps approached from the other side of the door and a young man in his early 20s peered at Bertolli as the door was swung open. "Yes, what is it?"

"Oh hello, I'm a friend of Amy McNaught next door. Sorry to disturb you, but I was passing by and thought I'd drop in to see Amy as I haven't seen her in a while. I just went to knock on her door and noticed that all the curtains are drawn. Do you know if she's away?"

The young man looked nervously at Bertolli and began to stutter in his reply. "Erm...how do you...erm... know Ms McNaught? I don't know... if I... should be speaking... to you." Bertolli could understand why the young man saw him as suspicious, but he was determined to remain anonymous and not to let the cat out of the bag concerning a police presence. Bertolli smiled, said something indistinct, turned on his heels and walked away.

Once safely in the haven of the Capri, Bertolli called DCI Gravesham to inform her of the latest developments. He asked her to approve a stake-out of 821 so that plain-clothes police officers could keep an eye on the house twenty-four hours a day. She agreed with his request and ordered him to stay in the vicinity until 6.00 p.m., when another officer would take over from him. Bertolli moved his car to a closer parking space and ensured he had a good view of the entrance to 821 in his right-hand wing-mirror.

The stake-out of 821 Burrage Road was now in its fifth day and the only person seen approaching the premises during this entire time was the postal worker delivering mail. Bertolli was now on his third watch of the property and beginning to experience that old familiar feeling that things were not going to work out the way he had hoped. He was now so fed up with the case that he couldn't wait for this shift to end so that he could go home and have a nice cool beer. Just twenty-three minutes to go and he'd be on his way home.

The next twenty-three minutes seemed to pass very slowly as Bertolli contemplated the implications for his career of yet another failed attempt to nail Mr Sheen. DCI Gravesham already had a low opinion of him even though previously he'd had an excellent record in solving serious cases. She saw in Bertolli everything she detested...a loner who thought he was too clever for the others and who led a shambolic life like some university student. Gravesham liked her officers to dress smartly, be on time, think in a predictable way and be team-players. Bertolli inserted the key into the ignition as he battled with his defeatist thoughts. He leaned his arm over the back of the driver's seat to check for traffic and fired up the Capri's noisy engine. Just as he was about to pull off, his eye was drawn to a glint reflected in his wing-mirror. He turned off the engine as he looked closely at the image in his wing-mirror: a man in the distance carrying something that was glinting in the sun. The image grew as the man got closer to the car until his appearance was revealed: a thin short-haired man of moderate height with a navy blue fleece jacket and jeans. This looked just like the man that Paul Kanner had described coming out of 47 Granby Street...and he was carrying a bulky-looking orange Sainsbury's carrier bag that had a metal canister of some sort at the top! It had to be him. It had to be Mr Sheen! Bertolli slapped his steering wheel with joy as the image of the man disappeared from view.

Joe Bertolli called for backup over his phone before easing himself gently out of his car. He walked slowly towards 821 and lingered at the edge of the driveway. Proper procedure would be to wait for backup before attempting to investigate, but he wanted to make a quick assessment of the situation before his colleagues arrived. He strolled as casually as he could manage up to the front door, all the while keeping his growing sense of excitement in check. Should he need an excuse for explaining his visit, he would use the same story that he had used with the young man next door: that he was dropping by to see his friend Amy McNaught. Now that he was very close to the front window of the house, Bertolli could make out a glimmer of light through the curtains. He stepped back a few paces and noticed a human silhouette bobbing up and down. It had to be Mr Sheen...maybe he was bending down to pick up dust with his duster and then straightening up again to scrape the dust into some kind of container.

After a couple of minutes of indecision, Bertolli retraced his steps to the front of the driveway where he could get a better view of the upstairs window. There was now no doubt in his mind: Mr Sheen was up there and he was repeatedly bending down and straightening up every few seconds. It occurred to Bertolli that the house must have already been burgled recently because Mr Sheen must be on his second visit here, as he saw the man carrying only a carrier bag. There was definitely no sign of the kind of large lorry that would be needed to accommodate the furniture that would be contained in a house of this size. He decided to hang around the driveway until his reinforcements arrived. Suddenly, the front door opened and a man emerged with an orange carrier bag. The man turned his back on Bertolli as he tried to lock the front door of 821 with a key. Bertolli had to think quickly and change his plan.

Bertolli ambled nonchalantly towards the man at the front door and spoke to him in a steady voice. "Hello, are you John McNaught by any chance? I'm just over from New Zealand and was hoping to catch Amy before I fly back in a couple of days."

The man gave Bertolli an appraising look and forced a smile. "Oh, a friend of Amy's? How do you do? I'm a colleague of hers...she asked me to water her houseplants and do a bit of dusting while she's away. It's a shame that you've missed her."

Bertolli realised that he was dealing with a clever and flexible criminal. "So, when did she leave?"

"Just over a week ago. Not sure when she'll be returning though. She has taken six months' leave from work, but she might decide to return home sooner. She said she'd let me know."

"What a pity. I haven't seen her in close to five years and I'd hoped I'd catch her before I left. Do you mind letting me into the house so that I can leave a message for her?"

Mr Sheen narrowed his eyes as he tried to formulate an answer. "Look, why don't you write a note and put it through the letter box? I'm running late for an appointment and have to get off." Before Bertolli could utter a reply, the man started to walk along the drive.

"Excuse me...can you hold on just a sec? I think I saw something move behind the window just now. Let's quickly go in and check in case a stray cat has wandered in there." Bertolli was trying to buy time in the hope that his reinforcements would arrive.

"Let's take a look through the window then. After you...show me where you saw this cat."

Bertolli peered through the large bay window and was just about to turn round when he very suddenly lost consciousness. Mr Sheen had hit him on the back of the head with his canister of furniture spray! After some minutes, he slowly regained consciousness and tried unsuccessfully to stand up. Still lying on the ground, he could see Mr Sheen sandwiched between two uniformed policemen, one of whom was trying to place handcuffs on him. Before he had time to speak, Bertolli saw an ambulance pull up. He tried to get to his feet again and this time succeeded. Staggering like a drunk with his head in his hands, he told the paramedics that he was OK and didn't need to go to hospital. After a quick check of his vital signs, the paramedics drove away just as Mr Sheen was being escorted to the waiting squad car. Joe Bertolli called to the policeman entering the passenger side of the car and told him to search Mr Sheen for the key to the front door. The policeman handed Bertolli a skeleton key, saying that it was the only key they found on the intruder.

Now alone, Bertolli shakily approached the front door and jiggled the skeleton key in an attempt to open the front door. After two minutes, the lock made a clicking sound and Bertolli pushed the door open. He turned on the hallway light and then entered the room on the right. He smiled as he read the words painted in large red letters on one of the walls:-

You will read about my message

in the newspapers

You know I'm after you

You know what I want

I will never stop

    Satisfied that Mr Sheen was finally caught, Joe Bertolli jumped into the Capri and sped to Greenwich Police Station. He couldn't wait to find out about Mr Sheen's true identity and motives.

-Chapter 17-

Revelations

Sgt Joe Bertolli stood behind the one-way mirror and observed the progress of the interview. Normally, as the principal investigating officer, he would be conducting the interview himself. However, his head was still throbbing from the blow to his head and DCI Gravesham insisted that she would conduct the interview personally, with the assistance of Detective Constable Mike Chandler.

It emerged that the real name of Mr Sheen was Ralph Cartwright, a former Captain in the British Army, who had fallen on hard times after his last tour of duty in Afghanistan. The nerve-wracking war against the Taliban had taken its toll on his mental health and led to an increasing reliance on alcohol to get him through the day. Just as he had completed a residential week in therapy for his alcohol problems, his whole world fell apart. He came home to an empty house...literally stripped of furnishings and everything else. Most significantly, his wife Amy and year-old son Patrick were nowhere to be seen. He called on Amy's parents, only to be told that Amy and Patrick had moved to some big house in South-East London and were living with a wealthy Scotsman called John Mac-something or Mc-something. He also went by the name of Jack and sometimes Amy had referred to him as Jock. Ralph Cartwright was completely overwhelmed by these revelations and couldn't get his head round this unexpected and apparently sudden change in his fortunes. But one day it dawned on him...he remembered that Amy had mentioned a wealthy Scottish friend who went abroad a lot.

The devastating news of his wife's desertion

had led to Ralph Cartwright's mind spiralling out of control and he returned to heavy drinking. He had resorted to mugging and stealing at every opportunity in order to feed his alcoholism and was eventually caught after he attempted to burgle a flat in North London. Whilst serving his prison sentence, he had formulated his plan for getting his son back. He planned to scope Amy's parents' house as he knew that Amy would more than likely be visiting them and would be taking Patrick with her. When he came out of prison, he discovered that Amy's parents' house was occupied by strangers and he couldn't track them down. It was then time for Plan B: all he had to go on was what Amy's parents had told him that last time he had spoken to them.

Ralph Cartwright's revelations fit well with what Paul Kanner, Benjamin Zeigarnik and Joe Bertolli had surmised: 'Mr Sheen' gave the houses he'd burgled a thorough clean in the hope of collecting samples of DNA. He would pass these on to an old school friend of his who was an out-of-work molecular biologist, in the hope that there'd be a match with the DNA obtained from a locket of his son's hair that he'd kept.

As the interview drew to a close, Ralph Cartwright dissolved into a flood of tears. "I just cannot deal with this any longer. I haven't seen my son in twelve years. My baby boy is now a teenager and he doesn't even know I exist. Now I'll be serving time for the burglaries...it was all for nothing. Where do I go from here?"

Joe Bertolli continued to watch the distraught former army captain through the one- way mirror. He felt an empathic sadness for this man's plight, with echoes from his own life.

-Chapter 18-

Case Closed

Joe Bertolli arranged to meet Benjamin Zeigarnik and Paul Kanner for a celebratory get-together and for an opportunity to inform them of how the case of Mr Sheen finally played out. He picked up Paul from Bertram Street and drove him to Café Roma in Bloomsbury, where Zeigarnik was already waiting for them at a table he had booked for the three of them.

"Before Benjamin comes up with any of his bad jokes, I'd just like to thank you both for helping me to solve this case. I admit that there's no way I could have solved it without your two." Zeigarnik raised his eyebrows in mock horror and Paul smiled in a way that neither man had seen before: a smile of satisfaction, bordering on a smirk!

The happy spell they had all fallen under was suddenly broken. "It was a bitter-sweet victory my friends" uttered Zeigarnik in a grave voice. "Like you Joe, I feel for this man, even though he was a criminal. Life sometimes deals us an unfair hand. This Ralph Cartwright seems as much a victim of life as a criminal." Bertolli bobbed his head up and down in agreement and was about to start speaking when he checked himself. Both Zeigarnik and Paul looked expectantly towards him.

"Er...well, I wasn't really going to tell you about this, but I kind of bent the rules a bit to ease Cartwright's pain. I managed to track down his ex-wife Amy through the Inland Revenue Database and explained the damage that her desertion had caused. She was surprisingly sympathetic and told me the reason that she disappeared with baby Patrick was because she feared Cartwright's violent outbursts and their effect on their young child. I gave her Cartwright's prison address and she promised me that she'd write to him, explaining her reasons. She even told me that she'd arrange a video-call between Cartwright and thirteen-year-old Patrick if she was assured that he could accept that she and Patrick would remain with her new partner. I don't know how things will pan out...hopefully, Ralph Cartwright and Patrick will be able to form some kind of bond which will be good for them both."

Benjamin Zeigarnik and Paul Kanner looked at Joe Bertolli as if for the first time. Zeigarnik discerned sentiments he'd never before seen expressed in his friend, whereas Paul was simply surprised by the calmness in Joe's voice.

Bertolli reached into his back-pack and gazed at Paul. "Paul, this is for you...for all your help. You've been amazing!"

Paul's eyes widened as he was handed an

ornate wooden box. He opened it and marvelled at the contents: a replica set of the Lewis Chessmen pieces carved from light and dark wood. Paul knew a little of the story behind the original chess pieces. These were discovered in the 19th century in the Outer Hebrides in Scotland and were believed to belong to Nordic traders from the 12th century. "Wow, how amazing! Thank you!"

Finally, the food arrived. Dr Benjamin Zeigarnik gazed fondly at Sgt Joe Bertolli and the young Paul Kanner and uttered his favourite words: "Eat, eat!" He then reached out and tapped Paul lightly on the arm: "I think I may have a need of your services in the near future young Paul, even if Joe here doesn't want to play cops and robbers anymore!"

Connections

Most young people who have read this book won't be interested in following up background material, but if you are a curious young person or a curious older reader who has strayed into this territory, you might be interested to know about some of the material that indirectly or directly has a bearing on this story:-

Paul Kanner's name was derived from Dr Leo Kanner, the Austrian-American child psychiatrist who first identified child autism in 1943. A clear account of the man and his work is available in this article:

> Cohmer, S. (2014). Autistic disturbances of affective contact (1943), by Leo Kanner. http://embryo.asu.edu/handle/10776/789
> 5

Paul has Asperger's Syndrome, which shares some features with autism. This is named after Hans Asperger, an Austrian Paediatrician who identified the syndrome in 1944. His life has been surrounded by controversy, with some accounts lauding him as a saviour of children during the Nazi atrocities while others have implicated him as a Nazi collaborator:

Czech, H. (2018), Hans Asperger, national socialism, and 'race hygiene' in Nazi-era Vienna. *Molecular Autism, 9:29.*

For accounts of psychological characteristics of people with Asperger's Syndrome:

Robison, J.E. (2007). *Look Me in the Eye*. NY: Crown Books.

For children: Jennifer Cook O'Toole's *The Asperkid's (Secret) Book of Social Rules*, published by Jessica Kingsley Publishers.

Dr Benjamin Zeigarnik was named after Dr Bluma Zeigarnik, a psychologist who had studied and qualified in Berlin before returning to her homeland in the Soviet Union, where she worked in various university departments, clinics and research institutes. She was affiliated with Moscow State University until 1988, the year of her death, aged 81! She was a pioneer in the fields of memory research and clinical psychology in the 1920s and 1930s and has a very memorable Russian-sounding name! I see Benjamin as a fictional grandson of Bluma. Accounts of her life and work can be found in:

(1) Zeigarnik, A.V. (2007). Bluma Zeigarnik: A memoir. *Gestalt Theory, 29(3)*, 256-268.

(2) Seifert, C.M., & Patalano, A.L. (1991). Memory for incomplete tasks: A re-examination of the Zeigarnik effect. *Proceedings of the Thirteenth Annual Conference of the Cognitive Science Society.*

https://www.researcgate.net/publication/254731324.

Background on the colourful history of the polygraph test, including the psychologist Dr William Moulton Marston, who created *Wonder Woman*, and on other gadgets in Dr Benjamin Zeigarnik's lab can be found in:

(1) Lepore, J. (2014). *The Secret History of Wonder Woman*. London: Scribe.

(2) *Professor Marston and the Wonder Women.* (Film directed by Angela Robinson, released in 2017.)

(3) Tarase, G.M. et al. (2013). Scientific and legal procedure of polygraph test. *Journal of Biological Innovation, 2(1)*, 5-16.

(4) Teplan, M. (2002). Fundamentals of EEG measurement. *Measurement Science Review, 2(2)*.

For children: (1) Steve Korté's *What is the Story of Wonder Woman*, published by Penguin Workshop; (2) Crispin Boyer's *That's Sneaky: Stealthy Secrets and Devious Data that will Test your Lie Detector*, published by National Geographic Kids'.

Background on the psychological experiments in which Paul Kanner participated can be found in:

McCrory, E., et al. (2007). Eye-witness memory and suggestibility in children with Asperger syndrome. *Journal of Child Psychology and Psychiatry, 48(5)*, 482-489.

Simons, D.J., & Chabris, C.F. (1999). Gorillas in our midst: Sustained inattention blindness for dynamic events. *Perception, 28,* 1059-1074.

Swettenham, J., et al. (2014). Seeing the unseen: Autism involves reduced susceptibility to inattention blindness. *Neuropsychology, 28(4),* 563-570.

The practice of DNA profiling is explained in: *Forensic DNA Analysis: A Primer for Courts.* Royal Society and Royal Society of Edinburgh.

Basics for children: (1) Fran Balkwill and Mic Rolph's *Have a Nice DNA*, published by Cold Spring Harbour Laboratory Press; (2) Mandy Hartley's *The DNA Detectives: To Catch a Thief*, or her second book, *The DNA Detectives: The Smuggler's Daughter*, available via Amazon.

About the Author

Dr J D Demetre recently retired from his post of Principal Lecturer in Psychology at the University of Greenwich, London. He has held lectureships and research fellowships in Developmental Psychology at various universities and institutes in the UK and the US. He lives in South-East London. He is a long-suffering supporter of Charlton Athletic Football Club and when not pulling his hair out at football matches can be found leaning on a spade in a community garden, staring in his jam-jar ecosphere for any signs of life, trying to catch the family yorkiepoo or dodging the world from inside the covers of a book.

Printed in Great Britain
by Amazon